A Beth-H
Jacob Lai

Book 5:
The Sixth Stone

Jennifer St. Clair

Writers Exchange E-Publishing
http://www.writers-exchange.com

A Beth-Hill Novel: Jacob Lane Series, Book 5: The Sixth Stone
Copyright 2011, 2015 Jennifer St. Clair
Writers Exchange E-Publishing
PO Box 372
ATHERTON QLD 4883

Cover Art by: Jatin

Published by Writers Exchange E-Publishing
http://www.writers-exchange.com

Prologue

"Healers go where they are needed," Sennet said.

"You've said that before." Jacob sat down on the mis-matched couch and folded her arms. "What does that *mean?* Exactly?"

"I took you to meet Espen a week ago," Sennet said, joining Jacob on the couch. "Through the portal, not by mundane means. Why do you think we went that way?"

"Because--" It sounded stupid to say it out loud, but Jacob couldn't think of any other reason why they'd go through a portal and not in a car. "Because she lives too far away?"

Sennet smiled. "Yes and no," she said. "You could get into a car and drive for the rest of your life and still not find Espen's house."

"She lives in Faerie?" Jacob guessed.

"Not exactly, but you're closer," Sennet said. "What would you say if I told you that she doesn't live in this world at all? That there are other worlds--other realities--out there, where Healers can go if they are needed?"

Jacob sat and thought about that for a moment. Her first reaction was to deny it, but *Faerie* existed, after all. She couldn't deny that. And if Faerie existed, then why not other worlds? Why *not?*

"Does anyone else know about these other worlds?" she finally asked.

"They know, but they don't really think about them all that much," Sennet said. "There's enough trouble in this world, after all. And it's easier if you just go where you are needed and don't really worry about *where* you are. Or when."

"When?" Jacob asked. It wasn't that she hadn't learned a lot from the Healer; she had. But the suddenness of her talent appearing, and how she had saved Danny's life was still too new for the numbness to wear off. She hadn't quite gotten used to the fact that she was a 'Healer'--in training, yes, but a Healer nonetheless.

"Sometimes, yes," Sennet said, and a look passed across her face; a mixture of sadness and regret. "Hopefully, I'll be with you the first time you're called somewhere."

Jacob hoped so, too. She had none of Sennet's calm, none of her quiet strength.

"All you have to worry about is the person who called you, and that Healers are neutral," Sennet said. "If someone harms a Healer in the line of duty--"

"I've been meaning to ask you about that," Jacob said, thinking of Danny. "Why didn't the Healers withdraw when Genevieve was killed?"

"Danny's life and Gen's life were tangled together when he killed himself," Sennet said. "Someone had to sort it out, but not just anyone can approach a mess like that, much less make sense of what had happened."

"You're going to say that I was the only person who could have--" Jacob shook her head before she could finish the sentence. "I don't believe you. Stuff like that only happens in stories!"

"No. You were in the right place at the right time, that's all," Sennet said, and smiled. "It's not at all unusual."

This whole *conversation* was unusual. Jacob couldn't quite relax in the Healer's presence; she thought she would feel the same way if summoned to the private chambers of a Queen. Healers were important people, after all, quiet and resourceful, but *important*.

And Jacob was--well, just Jacob.

She'd tried to explain this to Sennet once, and the Healer had smiled, and nodded, and completely failed to understand. And then she'd taken Jacob out into the forest where a tiny little fairy had gotten caught in a spider web, and Jacob had cupped the fairy's body in her hand and she had healed the creature's broken wing--and for a moment, she had felt--different.

Almost--*connected.* To something more vast than the bulk of a dragon looming over her head.

She'd been too intrigued by the feeling to mention it to Sennet, and now, after weeks had passed without its mention, she hesitated to bring it up. But it wasn't ever far from her mind.

"What are you planning to do today?" she asked.

"I thought I'd take you shopping," Sennet said. "It's almost the holiday season, after all, and the holidays are stressful for most people. I want to show you something I think you'll enjoy."

So they had walked to the bus stop--Sennet didn't own a car--and they had taken the bus to the nearest mall, a world away from Darkbrook even though it was only--in truth--less than fifteen miles. Despite the fact that it was November, holiday music blared from the speaker, the stores were selling everything under the sun, and while the music spoke of peace and goodwill and happiness, Jacob only saw a handful of people who were actually smiling.

"Sometimes I come here just to people watch," Sennet said, and sat down on a nearby bench. She patted the seat beside her, and Jacob sat down. "To remind myself that there are other things than magic. That most of these people would never believe that the Wild Hunt once terrorized this town, or that Darkbrook actually exists."

"There are more people who are hurt in this world than one network of Healers can heal," Jacob said softly, watching a girl on crutches maneuver her way past two strollers piled high with bags and packages.

"We tend to stick to the fringes of what everyone else would call society. Those who cannot risk taking their wounded to a doctor--especially in this day and age--come to us. *We* don't ask questions." She smiled. "Well, not that many, and not always."

"If that girl came to you, would you heal her?" Jacob asked.

"Of course," Sennet replied. "But she wouldn't come to me, or to you either. And if you approached her and offered to heal her, what do you think would happen?"

There were--stories, after all. From places the Healers had withdrawn from; horrible stories of wards in which Healers were imprisoned and forced to heal well beyond the last reaches of their strength; well beyond their sanity.

Nowadays, according to Sennet, no Healer followed a call without informing another Healer of their whereabouts. There were portals for Healers to use, and no one was ever more than a call away. The advent of cell phones had helped a lot.

"And there are some things that healers cannot heal," Sennet said. "More things than you might think. We aren't omniscient. We aren't perfect, or infallible in any way."

"That's not what everyone seems to think," Jacob said.

"Yes, I've noticed that, especially recently. I'm not sure that's a good thing at all." Sennet nodded to a group of women huddled around a crying child. There were other children present; bored and restless, but their parents weren't paying them any attention. One little girl caught Jacob's gaze and smiled quizzically, almost as if she knew who Jacob was, but couldn't quite remember where she'd seen her before. "There are some things we can do for them," she said, and quite suddenly, the music changed.

It was still the same song; a familiar one Jacob had known since she was small. But there was something different about it now; something almost *glittering,* a sparkle of goodwill that buoyed the people around them and put a spring into their steps. Strangers held doors open for other shoppers. People waiting in line stood up straighter, and smiled. Two women, strangers until now, turned to each and started talking about cats. A man, who had been scowling at the lady with a cartload of books at the bookstore, actually helped her unload her cart without a single unkind word.

"You can't fix everyone, but you can make everyone feel a little better?" Jacob asked. The group of women had soothed the child, and three of the children now played on the concrete animals that stood in the middle of the mall. Someone had put a Santa hat on the giraffe and wrapped a long scarf around its neck.

"You also can't help those who don't want to be healed," Sennet said quietly. "Are you hungry?"

The music was back to normal now; no sign of glitter or sparkles anywhere. But as they walked away from the middle of the mall towards the food court, Jacob realized that the people weren't returning to their frustrations. Sennet had unlocked something inside of them; or awakened something that had been asleep, perhaps, and while Jacob knew the feeling wouldn't last forever, perhaps it would--at least--last the rest of the day.

"Watch," Sennet said, and waved her hand in front of Jacob's face. "Here is the best lesson you can learn from me or anyone else. Everyone--and *everything*--you encounter is connected."

A web of light sprang from Sennet's fingers and spread out to touch the people around them -the kids on the carousel; the baby asleep in a stroller almost toppling with the weight of bags; the old man sitting alone at a table, forking the last bit of rice from the Chinese restaurant into his mouth; the group of teenagers dressed all in black with chains and piercings and skin almost pale enough to pass as vampires.

"If you help one person and they are a good person, then they will, in turn, help someone else," Sennet said. "If you help one person and they are a *bad* person, all you can do is hope that the good will outweigh the bad. But each person you heal, each life you touch, will touch you in turn, and you will, perhaps, know more about that person than you ever wanted to know. That's not a bad thing. Healers are neutral for a reason."

Jacob stared around her at the light that connected each and every person she saw; one with the other, their auras--for want of a better word--merging as they passed, even if they did not speak to one another, and then separating again with some of their colors mixed as they moved on their way.

The only two people who were not connected to anyone else were--of course, she thought--Sennet and herself. Although there were tendrils, here and there, that formed a sort of mesh as Jacob watched.

"Healers aren't connected?"

"Healers stand *outside*," Sennet said, and from her tone of voice, Jacob realized that 'outside' meant quite a bit more than walking to the nearest door and stepping through it. "We are connected to each other. It isn't called a 'network' of Healers for nothing, you realize."

Jacob shook her head. "I *didn't* realize. No one said anything about all of this--" There was another person seated at one of the food court's tables who wasn't--at least at first--connected to anyone else, either. But as Jacob watched, that same glowing mesh appeared between Sennet and the lady at the table, and then Jacob found herself joined with them both.

Sennet smiled. "Ah, there she is," she said, and waved across the crowd to where Espen sat, looking more like royalty than an ordinary shopper. But there was a bag by her chair, and she had an actual *mug* of tea in one of her hands. She waved with the other hand, motioning them over.

"They serve tea here? In mugs?" Jacob asked, and wondered if anyone else thought that was suspicious.

"They serve tea here in mugs if you know where to find it," Espen said as clearly as if she stood next to Jacob. And then, as they joined her, Jacob saw another lady--another Healer she hadn't met--winding her way through the shoppers with a tray holding three mugs and a steaming teapot, which she poured with some finesse as soon as she reached the table.

"I'm Minerva," the other Healer said, and handed Jacob a mug of tea. "I'm visiting."

Minerva wore her pale--almost *white*--hair in a braid down her back, and a colorful scarf as a headband of sorts. She had elvish features, almost, but her ears weren't pointed like Kyren's--Jacob tried to imagine Kyren in a mall and had to hide a smile in her tea. Minerva's clothing didn't really fit in at a mall, either, but no one seemed to notice she wasn't wearing any shoes, and that her dress seemed more homespun than store-bought.

"I'm Jacob," she said. "Nice to meet you."

"It's always nice to meet a young Healer," Minerva said, and smiled at Jacob. "There are so *few* new Healers nowadays--"

"Hence the reason why periodic vacations are important," Espen said. "When is the last time you left your post?"

Minerva sat down. "Oh, it must have been at *least* a century," she said, waving away a hundred years as if it were a day. "But Bets is coming along quite nicely, and I thought now was as good of a time as ever." She smiled brightly and sipped her tea.

"Elizabeth is two or three years older than you," Sennet said before Jacob could ask. "And she's Minerva's apprentice. I'm sure you'll meet her one day."

"Where is your post?" Jacob asked, remembering what Sennet had said about Espen's house.

"Oh, it's far from here," Minerva said vaguely. "And a bit of a hot button site at the moment, although I never would have left Bets in charge if I thought she was in danger." She hesitated, glanced at Jacob, then asked, "Any word from--"

"No," Espen said, and it was the finality in her voice that caught Jacob's attention.

Jacob glanced at Sennet, who seemed a bit annoyed that Minerva had even asked. And she wondered what they weren't saying--any word from whom? Another Healer? Did she dare ask?

"There are *alternate* places, Jacob, different than the ones I've mentioned," Sennet said after a long moment of silence. "Places like this, only different in some special way. Many *hundreds* of places."

"And the person who hasn't sent word is in one of these places?" Jacob asked.

"In all usual circumstances, we don't cover the alternates," Espen said. "We work with the actuals; those worlds that exist in a bubble of their own, not the ones that are twisted copies of this one or another. Every once in a while, though, a Healer will contact us from one of those places. That's what happened years ago when Freda contacted me with a bit of a situation on her hands. We helped, and stayed in contact, but--"

"But you don't *live* in this world," Jacob said before she could stop herself. "Why did she contact you and not someone here?"

"Either way, where I live and this place are as similar as here and Faerie," Espen said. "There's not much difference. But in Freda's case, there's quite a large anomaly--"

"You know of the Wild Hunt, I presume?" Minerva asked before Espen could continue.

"Yes," Jacob said. "I've--spoken with them."

"You know they were bound by the Council a hundred years ago and recently freed from the binding," Espen said.

"Yes, and I know their names," Jacob replied. "Josiah comes to Darkbrook sometimes, to help my Uncle Lucas." She hesitated. What did you *call* the Master of the Wild Hunt? It didn't seem right to call him 'Gabriel'. "I have a standing invitation to visit their home. And--"

"Gabriel's daughter Erianthe has enrolled in Darkbrook," Sennet said. "I think she's supposed to start soon. And if you remember, Espen, I wasn't there to help you before. I think that was around the same time as the war."

Jacob opened her mouth to ask, but Espen spoke first.

"In Freda's world, the Hunt was never bound," she said. "The Council tried a hundred years ago, but they failed."

"They--they *failed?*" Jacob asked, and quite suddenly, the fact that they sat in the middle of a mall food court seemed all the more strange. "But--if the Hunt was never bound--"

She'd read the stories, after all. *Everyone* had. Some of the stories were obviously myth, but most of them held more than just a grain of truth. And once, not that long ago, she'd found the diary of her great-great-uncle Peter, who had been one of the Council members to attempt the binding, and one of the few to survive.

What would the world be like if the Hunt was never bound?

"We helped corral the Hunt," Espen said quietly, as if she sensed some of Jacob's thoughts. "We roped off the forest with magic; Darkbrook was abandoned, and the Hunt left to starve or fade away. No one was quite certain what would happen."

"Our spells have not failed, so we know they haven't escaped," Minerva said. "But we haven't heard from Freda for almost three months. And after weekly letters--"

"It does seem a bit suspicious," Espen admitted. "Even though there's a bit of a time lag between this world and that one."

"Darkbrook was *abandoned*?" Jacob repeated.

"Without a Council, that was really the only thing that could be done," Espen said, watching her closely. "We couldn't negotiate with someone willing to murder anyone who set foot in his path, after all." She smiled. "Don't worry about it, Jacob. That isn't *your* place, after all."

"But still--" Jacob didn't want to argue with a Healer, but she couldn't help it. Josiah was *nice*. Even Gabriel had not been a monster. And what about his daughter? What about *herself*? If there was no Council, was there no Jacob Lane in this alternate world? Or Uncle Lucas? Or her mother and father?

"If the Hunt exists in this other world, do *I* exist too?"

"I doubt it," Espen said. "The alternates tend to break off during some terrible struggle; perhaps in one, someone who died would then live, or vice versa. In this one, among other things, the Hunt was not bound. In some, wars were not fought or they were; kings were not murdered or they were. Do you understand?"

"It's like a nightmare," Jacob said. "Or a horror story. I *like* the Hunt. At least, the Hounds I've met."

"And there is no reason not to," Minerva said. "It's like a nightmare, yes, but it's also real. If you go looking for alternates, child, you'll find them, but its best to stick with what you have here."

But even after their conversation veered off into another direction, Jacob couldn't stop thinking about it. The Hunt, never bound. Or, bound to the forest, but Darkbrook *abandoned?* That was almost too terrible to contemplate.

And later, as she walked back to Darkbrook from Sennet's house, she wondered if another Jacob Lane in another alternate reality was walking home from someone's house, and maybe, just maybe, in one alternate world, her parents really *had* been killed by the dragons.

And maybe that thought was the worst of all.

Chapter One

A rlen had--somehow--broken off from the main body
of the hunt. For a while, he was content to ride by
himself and away from the others, despite what his
uncle had said was grave danger.

After all, it had been *weeks* since his uncle had brought back
a kill.

He heard the sounds of the rest of the party for the longest
time before he realized the noise had grown fainter and fainter
as his horse picked through the thick underbrush of the forest.

And even then, Arlen wasn't frightened until he reached a
wide creek--with a sturdy bridge across its width--and saw the
decaying bulk of what had to be Darkbrook standing alone in a
clearing, broken out windows glittering dully in what weak
sunlight managed to pierce the forest canopy.

Half the building had been smothered by ivy over the years; what remained free of ivy had been touched by fire sometime in the past century, but was largely intact.

Just the sight of the castle was enough to freeze Arlen into place--at least, until the Hound growled behind him and he remembered the hunt and why he was in the forest in the first place.

Arlen's breath caught in his throat. He fumbled for a weapon--his uncle had refused to allow the hunters to carry guns--but it was too late even then. It had been too late--probably--since he saw Darkbrook and realized how far he had come.

His horse was no help; it sat quiet and unperturbed as the Hound wrested the crossbow from Arlen's hands and pulled him to the ground. For a moment, with the Hound's knee on his back and the crossbow bolt cold against the back of his neck, Arlen breathed in leaf mold and dirt and wondered if his uncle would miss him once he was dead.

And then, the Hound's weight lifted from his back. Arlen did not dare move until he heard the creature curse. Even then, when he glanced up and saw the Hound standing over him with the crossbow in one hand and the horse's reins in the other, he found himself frozen in place, still waiting to die.

"Get up." The Hound's voice was perfectly modulated and completely civilized, a far reach from the picture of the ravening monsters his uncle had painted.

Arlen scrambled to his feet and stood in front of the Hound, panting and frightened, bracing himself for the cold steel of the crossbow bolt as it slid into his chest.

Or maybe the Hound would shoot him in the stomach and leave him to bleed to death on the forest floor.

"How did you get past--" the Hound broke off whatever he intended to say and shook his head. The crossbow wobbled in his hands. Arlen flinched.

"Walk," the Hound growled, and started forward. "If you try to run, I *will* shoot you."

"W...walk?" Arlen stuttered. "W...where?"

"To the castle, of course," the Hound said impatiently. "I believe you humans called it Darkbrook?"

Arlen stopped so quickly that he almost collided with the horse. "Inside?" He spoke without thinking. "But--*monsters* live inside Darkbrook!"

The Hound bowed, sardonically. "So they say."

Arlen stared at the Hound for a moment, panic casting out any remnants of sense. He fell to his knees. "Please...please don't eat me!"

The Hound snorted. "Don't be silly," he said. "Despite the stories you may have heard, we *don't* eat children."

Arlen staggered to his feet. "You don't?"

"Never once," the Hound said, and tugged on the horse's

reins. "Are you very fond of this horse?"

"What?" Arlen took a step backwards, closer to Darkbrook and his doom.

"The horse. Are you fond of the horse?"

"It's...it's my uncle's horse--"

The Hound nodded. "Good."

This time, when he started forward, Arlen managed to stay on his feet. "Good?" His voice barely quivered.

"We may not eat children, but we *do* have to eat," the Hound said, and motioned with his weapon. "Now *walk.*"

In a daze, Arlen let the Hound push him forward until--after no time at all--they stood in front of Darkbrook's double doors, locked and barred against everyone, especially the hunters.

The Hound prodded Arlen's back when he stopped again. "I would hate to shoot you," he said, far too polite for a *Hound.*

"But I...I had every intention of shooting *you,*" Arlen whispered, staring back at him.

The Hound's gaze went blank and cold. "I know."

"My uncle said--"

"Your uncle says we are beasts," a different voice said, and when Arlen turned around, a boy who seemed only a year or so older than him stood just inside the open doors, staring at him.

This Hound had blond hair and gray eyes and wore clothing just as worn as the other Hound's rags.

"I thought you were," Arlen whispered, and would have backed away if the older Hound had not prodded him forward.

As Arlen stumbled through the doorway, he heard a raucous cawing from behind them, in the forest, and watched as a cloud of crows billowed out of the treetops.

"The meadow," the older Hound said, sounding almost worried.

"They will *not* pass through our wards," the younger Hound said firmly, but the older Hound did not look convinced.

"Come with us, please," the younger Hound said. "We mean you no harm."

Arlen followed the younger Hound while the older one brought up the rear of the group. He had lowered the crossbow, at least; and he seemed much less frightening since he had not--yet--tried to eat Arlen *or* the horse.

There was a courtyard past the front doors and down a short hallway. The older Hound left the horse there, tied to a post.

"Why did you bring the horse?" the younger Hound asked.

"Meat," the older Hound said in a tone that brooked no argument. "And if they found an empty horse--"

The younger Hound nodded. "Point taken." He glanced at Arlen. "May we have your name?"

Arlen had to swallow twice before he could speak. "My

name is Arlen. Arlen--"

"Your uncle is Simon Parker," the older Hound said in a voice that said all bets were off; all promises forgotten.

Arlen did not ask how the Hounds could know such things while bound inside the forest, nor did he try to deny the truth. Instead, he held himself very still and tried not to flinch as the older Hound brought the crossbow up again. "Yes. He is."

"Robin, *don't*," the younger Hound said. *"Don't."*

"Give me one good reason why," the older Hound snarled, and the civility was gone now, the mask of politeness just that - a mask.

"Because it will not change anything," the younger Hound said. "He will still be dead."

"Dead--?" the older Hound whispered, and choked on his next breath. The crossbow wavered.

Arlen knew he wouldn't have a chance to live if he tried to wrest it away, so he held still, his hands empty, and closed his eyes. If he died in the next few minutes, he thought he would not rather see his death coming.

"He died an hour ago," the younger Hound said, and some bottomless sorrow rode the backs of his words now. "Kris is with him still."

"Don't give him our names!" the older Hound shouted, and Arlen heard him pull the trigger. He flinched back as something whooshed past his face--a spell?--and cracked open his eyes just in time to see the crossbow bolt clatter to the ground from where it had been hanging right in front of his face.

And for a very long minute, all he could do was gasp and gurgle as he tried to wrap his mind around the fact that one Hound had saved his life while the other one had sought to end it.

"You--" He managed to force one word out, at least, and backed against the wall as the younger Hound approached. The other Hound stood stock-still, as if he had been frozen, staring at something Arlen could not see.

Gently, the younger Hound removed the crossbow from the older Hound's slack grasp. He seemed to take care not to touch him, perhaps for fear of what would happen when he emerged from his daze.

The older Hound took a step backwards, blinked, and bared his teeth. And then, he shifted shape into a menacing white Hound, favored Arlen with a look of pure malice, and ran off down the hall.

No less than a minute later, Arlen heard the horse scream. He started forward, as if intending to follow the Hound, but the younger Hound stopped him.

"Let him have this death," he said.

Arlen stared at him. "Since you thwarted him of mine?"

The Hound shook his head. "He did not mean to kill you,"

he said. "And you don't understand what's going on."

"What *is* going on?" Arlen asked. "My uncle--"

"Your uncle is hunting us to extinction," the Hound said. "And we wish to negotiate our surrender."

"Your *surrender*?" Arlen repeated. "But--"

"It is either that or die," a new voice said, and a girl--an actual *girl*--appeared from another room, her eyes red-rimmed, but clear.

There was a streak of blood across one of her cheeks and blood on her hands, but she didn't seem to notice.

"We wish to negotiate our surrender to the Healers who bound us here," the younger Hound said.

Arlen stared at him. "But--your Master agrees to this? Why do you need *me*?"

"If one of us appeared to your uncle and declared our intent to surrender, what would happen?" the girl asked.

"He would--" Arlen felt sick. He would have liked to say that his uncle would have listened, but 'surrender' wasn't anywhere in his uncle's vocabulary. "He would kill you," he said miserably.

"The Healers are said to be honorable," the younger Hound said. "Would you contact a Healer on our behalf and deliver our request?"

He asked this as if Arlen had experience in this sort of thing, this negotiation of lives. And was there a hint of desperation in his voice? Neither Hound had mentioned their Master--was this a mutiny?

"What does your Master say about this?" he asked.

"Our Master is dead," the older Hound said from the end of the corridor. "Your uncle killed him eight months ago."

Arlen's uncle had suspected *something,* but he'd only worked in his methodical way to attempt to discern why no one had seen the Master of the Hunt for almost a year. He had boasted that the Hounds seemed easier to kill lately, and he'd even mentioned that they had become harder to find.

"How many of you are *left?*" Arlen asked.

The Hounds exchanged glances.

"We would prefer that your uncle not know that he is so close to his goal," the younger Hound said into the silence.

"There were four of us yesterday," the older Hound said.

"Now do you understand why we wish to surrender?" the younger Hound asked.

"Do you know the Healer?" the older Hound asked.

"I know her," Arlen said and folded his arms, suddenly cold. "Her name is Freda."

"Will you take her our request?" the younger Hound asked softly.

"Do I...do I have a choice?"

"I could have killed you," the older Hound said.

"You nearly did!" Arlen pointed out, his voice rising on the last word.

"But he did not, and you still live," the girl said. "And we will deliver you to the edge of the forest--safely--if you agree to do this for us."

"And if I refuse?" Arlen asked. "And if I agree, and then do not deliver your request?"

"If you refuse, we have failed and we will die," the younger Hound said. "If you agree, and then go back on your word, then we have failed and we will die."

He said this without emotion; without any sign of sadness. Just stating the bare bones of simple fact.

And perhaps it was this that convinced Arlen they were telling the truth. They didn't try to convince him, or debase themselves to beg. They only waited, patiently, for his decision, their fate in his hands.

"I will take your request to the Healer," Arlen said, and his voice barely shook.

The younger Hound stood for a moment with his eyes closed.

"Thank you," the girl said.

After a moment, the younger Hound pulled an envelope from his pocket and held it out for Arlen to take.

"This should convince the Healer that you are telling the truth," he said. "Our wards will allow the Healer inside--and you, if you decide to come with her."

Arlen opened his mouth to tell the Hounds that he had no intention of ever setting foot in the forest again, but he nodded instead and tucked the envelope away.

"You have wards," he said slowly, the fog around his brain struggling to dissipate as he finally began to believe they would not kill him. "But--wouldn't that make one of you a *wizard?*"

The younger Hound smiled faintly. "Yes. It would."

"And you cannot break through the Healer's binding?" Arlen asked.

"Not yet," the girl said. "And not now. Not if we can end this without shedding any more blood."

Arlen nodded. "I will deliver your request, then," he said, and then, since they had left him with his life, "My uncle--this is the last hunt for a week. My uncle is going away for a short time. He won't tell anyone where he is going."

"He won't tell *you,* you mean," the girl said.

"No one seems to know," Arlen replied. "I've asked."

"Then we have a week to end this," the younger Hound said. "You should go now, I think." He did something with his hands, grim-faced and silent, and a portal appeared in the doorway on the other side of the corridor, pulsing blue and green and gold.

"Go," the girl said, and took the younger Hound's arm as he faltered.

Arlen hesitated. "Is he--"

The younger Hound's eyes slid shut and he sagged in the girl's arms.

"It is too much for him to hold at once!" the older Hound shouted and appeared beside Arlen, his teeth bared. "Go!"

With one last glance back at the three Hounds, Arlen stepped through the portal and fell to his knees onto the forest floor, where he stayed, huddled and shaking, until he heard the sound of horses behind him, and then, after a moment, his uncle's voice.

"Where is your horse?"

Arlen glanced up at him. "There--there was a Hound--"

The two men behind his uncle broke away from the group; the others stayed.

"The Hound is gone," Arlen whispered. "He took--he took the horse--"

"*It*," his uncle snapped.

Arlen stared up at him, confused. "What?"

"Are you wounded, boy?" one of the other men asked.

"N...no, I--" Arlen wobbled to his feet. "I think I hit my head," he said, which wasn't the truth, but might get him to see the Healer sooner.

"You should not have brought him," one of the other men said.

Arlen's uncle ignored him. "And your weapon?"

"H...he took that, too," Arlen whispered, and burst into

tears.

Disgusted, Arlen's uncle spurred his horse past his nephew. One of the other men stopped, and helped Arlen onto the back of his horse, and he sat there, sniveling and shivering as the hunting party moved out of the forest, past the boundary and into civilization again.

Arlen's uncle did not speak, but Arlen felt his fury from the front of the group and dreaded the thought of facing his uncle at home.

But at least they didn't refuse to deliver him to the Healer, and he did not have to pretend to cry when she enveloped him into her arms and led him into the safety of her house, away from Hounds and hunting and the last desperate plea of the dying.

S ometime later, Arlen awoke with a start, gasping, the crossbow bolt in front of him again, hanging--deadly and sleek--in midair.

"You've had quite a shock, or so I'm told," a soft voice said from the other side of the room. "How do you feel?"

The envelope was pressed against his side, so the Healer had not taken it. Arlen didn't remember falling asleep, but he lay on a couch near a crackling fire with a quilt cocooning him in warmth.

"I...I'm fine," he said, and pushed himself up. He glanced around the cluttered room, trying to figure out if his uncle or someone else waited in the wings, but he saw no sign of another person. "How long was I asleep?"

"No more than a few hours," the Healer said, and he saw

her now, sitting in a plumply upholstered chair with a basket of wool in her lap. "I'm to ring for a car when you're ready to go home."

Arlen shivered and closed his eyes.

"If you'd prefer to be ill for a day or so, I could arrange that as well," the Healer offered. "What happened out there in the forest? The man who brought you here said--"

"I told them a Hound stole my horse," Arlen said. "Is there anyone else here?"

"No one but us," the Healer said. "And no spells to spy on anything you might say, either." She waited a bit, then continued when he didn't speak. "Your name is Arlen Parker. I don't believe we've met officially, but my name is Freda."

Arlen fumbled in his pocket for the envelope. "I'm to give you this," he said, and held it out. "The Hounds wish to--to negotiate surrender with the Healers."

In silence, Freda set the basket of wool aside, took the envelope, and opened it. Inside were a few pages covered in handwriting--*old* paper, Arlen noticed, crumbling along the edges.

When she finished reading, she sat for a moment, lost in thought, and then just as carefully, folded the sheets of paper again and slid them back into the envelope.

"Did you read this?" she asked.

Arlen shook his head.

"And they spoke to you?"

"They could have killed me very easily, but they did not," Arlen said. "They spoke to me. They...they intended to *eat* my horse."

"*Who* spoke to you?" Freda asked. "The Hounds or their Master?"

Arlen hesitated. "They told me their Master was dead."

"Does your uncle know?" Freda pounced on that last statement with a strange sense of urgency, as if Arlen's answer would be the crux of the entire problem.

"He doesn't know for certain, but he suspects, I think," Arlen said. "There are only three Hounds left."

Freda closed her eyes, picked up the envelope again, and held it close to her chest. "Do you know who wrote this?"

"They didn't give me their names, but the youngest Hound called the girl Hound Kris. And I think he called the other one Robin."

"You call him the youngest--why?" Freda asked.

Arlen shrugged. "He didn't seem to be very old," he said. "The youngest one looked like he was a little older than me."

"And was *he* their wizard?" Freda asked.

"Yes, he was," Arlen said. "He fashioned a portal to the edge of the forest--"

"From where?" Freda asked.

"From Darkbrook," Arlen said. "I think they live there."

"Three Hounds," Freda said.

"There were four yesterday, they said. But one died."

Freda pressed her lips together. "I see." She hesitated. "Are you to send word somehow?"

"They told me their wards would let you pass," Arlen said. "And me, too, if I wanted to go back."

"And do you?" Freda asked.

Arlen started to shake his head, but then he surprised himself by nodding. "Can you help them? Can you accept their surrender?"

"That part is not up to me to accept," Freda said. "At least not by myself. But I can take them before the other Healers and allow their request to be heard."

"My uncle intends to kill them all," Arlen said. "He won't accept their surrender."

"If the Healers accept their surrender, they won't be inside the binding for your uncle to find," Freda said, and stood up. "You should--" she stared at him for a moment. "You should stay here."

Arlen didn't want to imagine what might happen. "I know."

"You *could* stay here," Freda suggested. "And I could bring them back here with me if they'll come." She frowned. "At least--"

"I'll go with you," Arlen said, and scrambled up off the

couch.

Freda nodded. "Very well. We'll go through a portal, I think. It's safer that way, and less likely to attract attention. Follow me."

Arlen followed her down a short hallway to another, smaller room that housed a floor-to-ceiling mirror and little else but a few odd chairs. With one wave of her hand, Freda opened a portal in the mirror, but, unlike the Hound's portal, this one showed its destination; the brooding bulk of Darkbrook itself.

"The Hound opened his portal in a doorway, not a mirror," Arlen said, shivering at the sight of the dark forest. He should have known that night had fallen by now, but Freda had not told him how long he had been asleep.

"He did?" Freda frowned. "That takes a lot more power than he should have had. Are you ready? As far as I can tell, their wards *will* let us pass."

"I'm ready," Arlen said and stepped up beside her. Freda took his hand, and for the first time, Arlen noticed she held the envelope in her other hand.

"Stay near me, please," Freda said, and together they stepped through the mirror.

The first thing Arlen noticed was the smell of cooking meat that hung like a pall of smoke across the forest. The second was the silence, just like before.

It had only been a few hours--perhaps half a day, unless he'd slept a lot more than he thought--since Arlen had stood very near this place, but it seemed that years had passed.

They encountered no one as they walked up to Darkbrook's front door, but the smell of cooking intensified.

The door opened at Freda's touch. Arlen nodded at her glance, and followed her inside.

They walked unmolested down the hallway and into the courtyard where Arlen had last seen the horse.

Now, its carcass lay hacked into pieces, with a stack of wood standing ready beside it to feed to the fire that burned in the middle of the courtyard. A hunk of meat already hung over the fire, the source of the smell.

A flash of movement caught Arlen's eye, and he turned just in time to see the older Hound duck down behind the stack of wood.

Freda waited for a moment to see if the Hound would appear from his hiding place. When he did not, she crouched to feed the fire, then glanced at Arlen.

"We should wait here, I suppose."

"Is he--" Arlen motioned towards the woodpile.

"No, he's gone," Freda said. "No doubt he went to warn the others." She glanced around the silent courtyard. "Although, if he waits too long, his supper will burn."

Arlen had not looked around the courtyard before, but

now he noticed newly disturbed dirt near the far wall, a rectangle, just like more than a dozen others that were older and slightly sunken. He knew they were graves almost before he started to point to them, and beside him, someone who wasn't Freda calmly used a stick to poke the fire.

"They are all buried here," the younger Hound said quietly, and used a small knife to cut a sliver of meat away from the bone. He popped it into his mouth, chewed for a moment, then regarded them, both cautious and wary.

"Your Master as well?" Freda asked, her voice perfectly calm.

Arlen stared at the Hound. "How did you--"

"Our Master as well," the younger Hound said, and only a small quiver in his voice belied anything but utter calm. "And twenty-two Hounds."

"You cannot push past our binding?" Freda asked.

"No," the younger Hound said after a moment of silence. "I cannot."

"And your name?" Freda reached out to turn the meat, and the Hound flinched, despite his composure.

"Noah," he said, his voice rough.

"Noah Wellington," Freda said with some satisfaction. "You were a student here, a century ago."

"*That* person died here a century ago," the Hound--Noah--said. "I am a Hound now, and have been a

Hound since then."

"That does explain how the Hunt came to have a wizard," Freda said. "And the others?"

Noah stared past them, towards the other side of the courtyard, and Arlen saw the other Hounds standing there in the gloom, barely visible beyond the light of the fire.

"They believe I can save them," he whispered, and when he glanced back at Freda, there were tears in his eyes. "I wish to negotiate--"

"Your surrender, yes," Freda said. "And I cannot grant you absolution myself. You must realize that."

"We do not ask for absolution," the older Hound said from a safe distance. "We only ask for our lives."

Freda held out the envelope. "I cannot accept this," she said. "The *Healers* will not accept this. We have no wish to bind you to us."

"Then you might as well kill us now!" the girl cried. "Because if you do not, *his* uncle will!"

"You misunderstand," Freda said patiently. "I cannot free you from the binding myself. You must ask for your freedom from the Healers who set the binding, and I can take you to them. But the rest is up to you."

Noah's gaze was fixed on the envelope. "Twenty-two Hounds and our Master died for that," he whispered. "That is what you wanted, a hundred years ago."

"What we wanted was to stop the carnage," Freda said softly. "Your Master--"

"We could argue all night long and still be at odds," the older Hound said before she could finish.

Freda's lips twitched. "That's true. Here is my proposal, then. Come with me and Arlen, right here, right now, and I'll take you to meet with the other Healers. I will give you my word that we will not harm you; nor do we wish your deaths."

"We would have to trust you, then," Noah said.

"Yes. You would. Quite possibly just as much as you trusted Arlen."

"Or more," the girl said.

"Is it true, then, that Healers do not kill?" the older Hound asked the question with a hitch in his voice, as if afraid of the answer.

"That is true," Freda said easily. "Healers do not kill."

"Then why condone our destruction?" Noah asked, his voice shaking.

"Would your Master have negotiated with us?" Freda asked.

"No." The older Hound's voice cracked.

"No," Noah said. "He wouldn't have."

"May I have *your* names?" Freda asked, aiming her question at the other two Hounds.

"Kris," the girl offered.

The older Hound hesitated. "Robin." But he spoke as if unsure of his own name.

"Your *true* name?" Freda asked.

"I have no true name," the older Hound replied. "I was--I was no student here."

That probably meant that Robin was one of the original Hounds, Arlen thought. *With more blood on his hands than anyone else.* But Freda made no mention of the obvious.

"I could return tomorrow if you'd like some time to consider my offer," she said. "There will be no penalty for waiting, and that will give me a chance to contact the others."

"And Simon Parker could return to kill us while you are gone," Noah said. "I would rather not wait."

"Very well," Freda said. "My portal stands just outside your wards--unless you have portals of your own?"

Noah's head jerked up. "Not past your binding, but I can create one."

Robin started to speak, but then subsided, shaking his head as if he disagreed with Noah's words.

"I don't believe there's much of a chance there are watchers in the forest," Freda said. "And my portal already exists."

Noah nodded, and Arlen thought he looked a bit relieved.

"We'll go directly to another Healer's house," Freda said. "It's a bit of a hike through a forest not unlike this one, but you should be fine. I *will* need your word that you will do as I say, no matter how strange it may seem."

"You have our word," Noah said hoarsely, and the others nodded.

"Then unless you wish to eat first, shall we go?" Freda asked.

Robin glanced at the meat and swallowed convulsively. "I have eaten my fill." And from the way he spoke, Arlen wondered if he'd eaten it raw.

Noah sliced off another piece, then did something so the fire died, just like that. "We are ready."

Together, they ventured outside into the forest; Healer, human, and Hounds. The Hounds were nervous and wary, but Arlen didn't realize why until they reached the portal and a voice spoke from the trees.

"You would *dare* betray me?"

Arlen heard the trigger release and tried to push the nearest Hound out of the way, but the crossbow bolt did not seek out a Hound.

Freda staggered, one hand pressed against her stomach, the other outstretched to ward off some unseen foe. She fell to her knees as Robin tried to catch her and Arlen bit back a shriek as Kris pulled him to the ground.

For a moment, Noah stood alone, frozen in place, and then Arlen saw his uncle step out of the forest and level the crossbow at the Hound's chest.

Robin erupted from the ground as a Hound, with Kris right behind them, but they were headed towards Arlen's uncle and Arlen only had eyes for Noah. He pulled the Hound away as his uncle pulled the trigger, and Noah fell onto his back, staring in horror as Arlen felt--at first, he felt as if something had sucked the breath from his body, but the pain was not far behind and threatened to swallow him whole.

He didn't remember falling, but quite suddenly, he felt someone's arms cradling him as he tried his best to remember how to breathe.

"You would murder your own *son*?" Freda's voice scraped across the roaring silence. "You would dare to murder a Healer?"

"I murdered no one," Arlen's uncle said calmly. "All the men with me this morning knew that a Hound stole my son's weapon." He trained the crossbow on Robin, who had to be growling, even though Arlen could not hear him.

The portal still shone where Freda had left it, mere feet away, but it had changed somehow; the colors were different; more intense, or perhaps that was just the pain stealing Arlen's life away.

Freda's hand closed over Arlen's arm, and something passed between them; a surge of some power he was sure she could not afford to share. But it took most of the pain away, and when he raised his hand to touch the bolt sticking out of his chest, only the wound remained, bleeding, but perhaps not as bad as before.

Kris was the next to fall; Arlen's uncle fired at her first and then Robin, but Robin ducked and the bolt passed harmlessly over his head. But that gave him no opportunity to attack. Arlen's uncle was too quick, even for Hounds.

"Wait--" Noah gasped out the word as Arlen's uncle trained the crossbow on Robin again. "Wait--please--"

"And who are *you*?" Arlen's uncle snapped. "I've seen these two before--"

Arlen tried to speak; to claim Noah as a classmate or at least, human, but he couldn't find his voice. Freda's hand had fallen away by now; Robin had inched towards the portal, and Kris had not moved since Arlen's uncle had shot her.

Noah stood his ground, his hands loose with no sign of magic around him. But he had to have something in mind because he was a wizard--Arlen tasted blood in the back of his throat as he tried to speak one last time.

"Uncle, please--"

Freda's hand latched onto his arm just as Noah spoke, and Arlen saw the sparkle of the portal fall across his vision.

Noah spoke a spell and a ward at the same time; Arlen saw Kris' body move and his uncle swing around; his uncle pulled the trigger, but not at Kris, at Robin, who was poised to leap--

And suddenly, Arlen lay alone in the forest with birdsong around him and sunlight dazzling his eyes, even though it had been dark before. He blinked and tried to make sense of his surroundings, but only when he saw the sparkle of the portal and someone's arm sticking through it did he realize that he had--somehow--ended up on the other side.

Alone. In a strange place; another world.

He had no strength left to fight the darkness when it rose to carry him away.

Chapter Three

The werewolves' territory had always been off-limits, although only in the vaguest sense. No student would walk for hours through wilderness just to catch a glimpse of a werewolf when they could see them in class; the allure was just not there. In the winter, the path would have been impossible. In autumn, with the crunch of leaves under their feet and the sun shining through the trees, it was a pleasant hike.

Danny didn't talk much at first; Jacob let him find the path and lead her through the forest. "Did I tell you I asked your uncle's permission to ask you to go?" he finally asked.

"No, you didn't," Jacob said, surprised. "What did he say? Why did you ask?"

"He said he thought it was a good idea to go." He shot her

a glance she couldn't quite interpret. "And I asked because you're human, and I'm not." He adjusted the weight of his backpack and glanced up at the sun. "After what I've already done, do you think I shouldn't have asked him?"

"People tend not to." To pass the time, she told him about Jordan, and her uncle's reaction to that request--after the fact.

Danny shook his head. "I see your point," he said. "But I didn't think I could risk it." He smiled at her. "You have powerful friends, after all."

"How far does this forest reach?" Jacob asked, refusing to rise to the bait of just *which* of her friends were so powerful. "No one seems to know." In the human world, there was a town on the other side of the State Park that hid Darkbrook, and a lake in between. Jacob had heard the waterfall existed in both worlds, but she'd never seen the one in Faerie.

"Faerie is like a lot of little kingdoms," Danny said, and she thought he was a bit relieved to be talking about something else. "There are kings and queens of various bits and pieces, but a lot of wild territory as well. The forest is--well, it's probably as big as the United States. I'm sure there are other continents, too, but I've never gone that far."

"Are there other Veils?" Jacob asked.

"I had a friend once who passed through the Veil here and ended up in Ireland," Danny said. "So there have to be other Veils. Or something like the same thing, at least."

"How did your friend get home?" Jacob asked.

Danny stiffened, and at first, Jacob thought he wouldn't reply. But then he said, slowly, "He found a wizard willing to open a portal to send him back. It was a long time ago."

And then Jacob remembered that Danny hadn't been the only werewolf to die that night in the forest. He'd lost friends, too. Had that been one of them? There wasn't really any easy way to ask.

"It's pretty out here," she said, trying to change the subject to something less volatile. "I bet you wouldn't even miss the towns."

"We didn't visit often," Danny said, "but when we did, we probably acted like people who had never come down off the mountain. We had no clue what modern life was like when I was young. It was only later, right before--you know--that we started mingling with the humans at Darkbrook and everyone else." He frowned and glanced behind them. "Do you--can you tell if we're being followed?"

Jacob neither saw nor sensed anyone behind them in the forest, but that didn't really surprise her. Danny was a werewolf, after all, and he had a *much* better sense of smell than she did. "Are you *sure*?" she started to say, and then, a white Hound emerged from the forest behind them and shifted shape into--Jacob thought his name was Nathaniel, but she wasn't certain.

Hound and werewolf stared at each other for a long moment, and Jacob thought that Danny wasn't really surprised to find that they had been followed.

"Lucas didn't ask," the Hound said, as if anticipating Danny's question. "Josiah told me. I told him I would follow you to the border."

"We're past the border," Danny said. His voice was neither friendly nor unfriendly, but Jacob half-expected the Hound to growl. "You're--"

"Nathaniel," the Hound said. "I apologize for not announcing myself to you. I had every intention of turning back long before now."

Jacob was willing to accept that explanation, but Danny didn't seem to be convinced.

"You expected us to run into trouble?"

Nathaniel hesitated. "I know where you're going."

Danny closed his eyes. "You know where--you've *been* there?"

"No, but Amalea has. She heard about what happened to you. And how you returned."

"What did you expect to find?" Jacob asked when Danny did not respond. She didn't know who Amalea was; perhaps she was an elf, like Kyren.

"It's more like what I *want* to find," Danny said. "What I *expect* to find is nothing at all."

"Amalea said--" Nathaniel began.

"She would not come herself?" Danny asked, a trifle sharply.

"She did not think she would be welcomed," Nathaniel said. "But if you wish, I could fetch her. Elves and werewolves aren't on the best of terms." He said this without a single ounce of anger or uncertainty.

"Are they dead?" The question burst from Danny's lips before he could stop it.

"There are graves, or what seem to be graves," Nathaniel said softly. "But they are marked in a language Amalea does not know."

"How many?" Danny swayed, steadied himself, and didn't protest when Jacob took his arm.

"Six," Nathaniel said. "They are marked with stones, all in a row."

Some knowledge sprang into Danny's gaze, but he didn't speak for a moment. "Tall stones?" he finally asked.

"She did not say," Nathaniel said. "But you can ask her--"

"I'll see for myself soon enough," Danny said, and turned away from both Nathaniel and Jacob, his shoulders stiff and set.

Jacob glanced at Nathaniel, who had made no move to leave. "Are we in danger if we go there?"

"No. I don't think so," he said after a moment. "And I will

leave you to your task. But Amalea will speak with you if you wish."

"She doesn't know what happened to my family," Danny said, his voice soft and quiet.

"Do you?" Nathaniel asked curiously.

Danny took a deep breath. "I think so." He hesitated, then, as if he didn't want to divulge werewolf secrets to a Hound.

"I do not need to know," Nathaniel said.

"It's not uncommon knowledge," Danny said. "You know there are worlds other than the human world and Faerie, right?"

"I have heard of such," Nathaniel said, and Jacob nodded at Danny's glance.

"Sennet told me about them," she said, but didn't mention the world where the Hunt was never bound.

"If I am right, my family was exiled to one of those places in punishment for *my* crime," Danny said, and this time, his smile held no humor. "There are usually markers, telling others what happened and where they were exiled to. If I had lived, I would have--" He stopped, then, considering his words. "I think I would have been killed if I had lived. But I might have been exiled, too."

"Can you--*find* them?" Jacob asked. "And bring them back?"

"If my family was exiled, I shouldn't *be* here," Danny said.

"I should be--"

"Dead," Nathaniel said. "I've heard there are those who wish you still were. Rumors, only."

Danny nodded. "I've heard the same rumors. Would you mind asking Amalea if she will come? And tell me what she knows?"

"I do not mind," Nathaniel said. "We will meet you at the stones, then. It will take me some time to travel."

"We'll be careful," Jacob promised, and Nathaniel shifted back into a Hound and loped away.

Chapter Four

D anny waited until Nathaniel was gone, and then glanced at Jacob, his gaze troubled. "I didn't think anyone would care if I did this," he said softly. "I didn't think trying to find what happened to my family would be such a big deal. There wouldn't be any werewolf packs near where my family lived because--well, they would have moved away. I really thought it would be fairly safe."

"I don't think anyone thinks you shouldn't go," Jacob said. "But I haven't heard any rumors, so I'm probably not the best person to ask. But you told Josiah--he's probably worried about you."

"He--" Danny sighed. "I would like to consider Josiah my friend, but the other Hounds aren't very--"

"They're not overly friendly," Jacob said, which had been

her impression as well.

Danny smiled. "Yes. They're perfectly *polite,* but I get the impression they're just waiting for me to leave. Or they don't approve. Or something."

Jacob puzzled over Danny's words. Why wouldn't he just come out and say that he *considered* Josiah a friend? And then, she realized what he had meant by that. If Gabriel didn't want Josiah to be friends with a werewolf, Josiah would have no choice but to comply.

Did the Hunt *have* friends in the same sense that Ophelia was her friend, or Emma, or Ash, even?

"Jacob?" Danny asked, sounding worried. "I--"

"You thought you might find that your family had been exiled," Jacob said. "You knew that was a possibility, right?"

"Well, yes, but I didn't know," Danny said. "No one told me, so I thought I should find out myself."

"So now that you know, what will you do?" Jacob asked.

"I should try to find them," Danny said. "They don't deserve exile for something *I* did."

"And how would you go about finding them?" Jacob asked.

"The stones should give clues," Danny said. "That's probably why Nathaniel's--Amalea thought they were graves. They should be marked."

Jacob wondered if he'd been about to call Amalea an elf,

which could very well be taken as an insult coming from a werewolf, but she decided not to mention it. "The Healers can travel to the other worlds," she said. "Have you thought about asking Sennet for help?" And then, on the tail end of that thought, she wondered if he'd expected to ask *her* to send him to another world to find his family. "Or Gen?" But then, before he could reply, she remembered what Sennet had told her time and time again. "Healers travel to where they are *needed.*"

"And if my family isn't in need of a Healer, would they be able to go there?" Danny asked.

"I don't know," Jacob admitted. "Probably not. But at the very least, they might be able to get a message to your family. It would be worth a try."

"Let's go to the stones first, and then we'll see," Danny asked. "But I have to ask--do you still want to come?"

"Of course!" Jacob said. "I told you I would. Did you think I wouldn't want to?"

Danny hesitated, then nodded. "I thought maybe you'd want to go back. Because I don't know what will happen if I try to open the way to where my family was exiled."

"Nathaniel and Amalea will be coming," Jacob said. "If you have to go, you have to go. I understand. And I'm *not* walking all the way back by myself."

Danny nodded. "Thank you."

In silence, they made their way through the forest, alert for any sound of pursuit. And when they reached the sunny glade that marked the spot where Danny's family had lived ten years before, no one was there to meet them.

As Nathaniel had said, there were six stones standing in front of the mouth of the cave. Six stones, carved with symbols Jacob couldn't read. Danny ran his fingers across the symbols on the tallest stone, then frowned.

"I smell--"

Someone moaned, not very far away, as if in response to Danny's voice. Jacob stiffened, because she felt a life in pain; a person in need--not a werewolf, she thought, but a *human*. Out here?

"Blood," Danny said, and turned around.

Twenty yards or so away, almost hidden in the space between two trees, was a portal. And in front of the portal lay a boy no older than Jacob, eyes closed, face pale, the front of his shirt drenched in blood.

Danny grabbed Jacob's arm as she moved past him. "Wait! It could be dangerous--"

"For that boy, yes," Jacob said. "You forget, I'm a Healer. I have to help him."

"Who would create a portal out *here*?" Danny followed her to the boy's side, then grabbed her arm again as she let her talent loose on the boy's wound. "Jacob, look at the portal."

His voice sounded strangled.

Jacob glanced up at the portal. At first, she didn't see what had Danny so upset, but then she saw the arm--a *woman's* arm--sticking out of the bottom of it, lifeless and still.

"That's the only thing keeping the portal in place," Jacob said softly. "Is she dead?"

"She--how am *I* supposed to know?" Danny asked. "What about *him*?"

"He'll be fine," Jacob said, and glanced down at her patient. "But I have *no* idea where he came from--"

The boy moaned again, but did not awaken.

"What if--what if whatever hurt him comes through the portal?" Danny asked, and slowly moved towards the portal, as if he expected the arm to come alive. But it didn't; it just lay there, neatly bisected by the portal, and when he lifted the limp wrist to test for a pulse, nothing happened.

"What if the arm belongs to the person who hurt him?" Jacob replied, but that didn't feel right. Even from this far away, she felt something familiar about the person who belonged to the arm, but she didn't know why. "Let me finish with him first. If anyone comes through the portal, or tries to, let me know."

"I don't think you can help whoever this is," Danny said, and moved away to stand guard over Jacob and the boy.

As Jacob healed the boy, his color improved and the pallor

left his cheeks. His eyes fluttered open once or twice, but he didn't really wake up until Danny's shadow fell across his face and he opened his eyes with a strangled shout.

"Hush," Jacob said gently. "You're--safe." *Safe enough,* she thought as the boy's gaze fastened on hers. "What is your name?"

He coughed and glanced wildly around. "Where--" He saw the portal. "Oh."

"Your name?" Danny pressed.

"My name is Arlen." The boy's eyes filled with tears, but he didn't cry. He raised one hand to touch the blood on his chest, shivered, and stared at Jacob again. "You're a Healer?"

"I'm an apprentice still, but yes," Jacob said. "I'm a Healer." She helped him sit up and lean against a nearby tree. "Do you know whose arm that is?"

Arlen nodded. "Her name is--was--Freda. Is she dead?"

"I think so," Danny said. "I can't feel her pulse."

"She was a Healer, too," Arlen whispered, and covered his face with his hands.

Jacob stared at the limp arm with its mundane sleeve and pale white fingers. *A Healer? Dead?* She had to contact Sennet, or Espen, or--She almost forgot about Danny, or how he might react.

"This was not your doing," she said as Danny stiffened. "You had nothing to do with this."

"I know," Danny murmured, "but it's still a shock."

"My uncle--" Arlen rubbed his hands across his face. "I need help. Freda was intending to bring the Hounds here to speak with the other Healers, but my uncle found us first. They may still be alive. Can you help me?"

"You're in no shape to go back through that portal and see what your uncle left behind," Danny said. "What are these Hounds?" He glanced at Jacob as he said this, and she saw a question in his gaze.

Arlen didn't mean the Hounds of the Wild Hunt; that much was obvious. And Jacob didn't recognize the Healers name--or did she? Hadn't Minerva asked Espen and Sennet about a Healer named Freda? Was this the same one? How many Healers named Freda *were* there?

"The place you are from--was the Hunt bound inside the forest? And they abandoned Darkbrook?"

Arlen stared at her as if she had grown an extra head. "Yes--you *know* where I am from?"

Danny only looked mystified. "Where is there a place where the Hunt was--"

"There are other worlds, remember?" Jacob asked him. "Like where your family was exiled. In this world, the Hunt was never bound to the Council. Espen called it an alternate world, not an actual."

"It's actual enough for the people who live there," Arlen

said, and wiped his face again. "But you know about the Hunt--do you know that the Hounds asked to surrender?"

"I don't know anything about that," Jacob said. "Why don't you tell us?"

Laboriously, Arlen worked his way through the terrible story in bits and pieces, some of which made no sense at all to Jacob, but obviously meant perfect sense to Arlen. Jacob felt a little strange to realize that the other Gabriel--or, the other Master of the Hunt, at least--was dead; Gabriel himself seemed ageless to her, unchanging like his Hounds.

"I think one of the Hounds is dead--that was Kris," Arlen whispered. "But Robin may be dead as well. My uncle could have left them to die--"

"No offense, but your uncle doesn't sound like the sort of person to leave someone else to die," Danny said. "He sounds like the type who would wait around to make sure they were dead."

"But he hasn't tried to come through the portal," Arlen said, then blanched. "Has he?"

"Not that we've seen," Jacob said. "Did he know where the portal led? And Freda was intending to bring you and the Hounds here to talk to Sennet and the other Healers?"

"She didn't name any names," Arlen said, "But that's what she said. She said the Healers had to accept their surrender and that she couldn't accept it herself."

She probably didn't want to leave them there where they would be killed, Jacob thought, but didn't say that out loud. "And your uncle was hunting them?"

"Noah--that's one of the Hounds--said that my uncle had killed twenty-two Hounds and their Master," Arlen said. "There were three left. Now--they might *all* be dead. My uncle said--"

"The portal is still open," Danny said softly.

"What do you think Sennet would say if I went through by myself?" Jacob asked. "What do you think Uncle Lucas would say?" And yet, could she make the long trek back to Sennet's house to tell her what had happened and leave the Hounds to die?

"I'll go," Arlen said, and tried to stand up. He didn't quite make it; his legs would not hold him.

"No," Danny said. "I've been healed enough times to know that you won't regain your strength for a little while. You stay here. I'll go."

"And what if you don't come back?" Jacob asked.

"I won't go far," Danny said. "I'll look for wounded, or bodies, and pull any survivors back through the portal. How long will it stay open?"

"I don't know," Jacob said, and moved to kneel in front of it so she could touch Freda's hand. "It shouldn't be open at all."

"Jacob--" Danny grabbed her hand just as the portal surged

through the connection Jacob had made. She gasped and tried to release Freda's hand, but the damage had already been done. In the time it took to blink, she knelt beside a woman's *body,* not just an arm, with Danny behind her and the portal gone.

"What just happened?" Danny demanded, swinging around, as if he expected to find the portal hiding behind one of the close-set trees.

It was night here, too, which didn't help. Jacob sat very still for a moment, staring down at Freda's slack face, wondering about the crossbow bolt in her lower chest. That hadn't been a very nice way to die, not that there *were* really any nice ways to die.

And this forest seemed--older, somehow. Untouched. But silent, with no creatures scurrying through the underbrush, no nightbirds calling in the trees. No crickets, even. Jacob's ears rang with the absence of sound.

"There's a body over here," Danny said quietly, his panic gone.

"That would be Kris, I'd expect," Jacob said. "One of the Hounds." She stood up and dusted her hands off on her jeans. "I can't open a portal to get us back, Danny." She felt tears gather in her eyes, and furiously blinked them away. "I don't know how to do portals yet. We haven't learned. And I'm not supposed to be an actual member of the Healer's network until after I graduate from Darkbrook, because there are rules for that, too."

Danny hesitated. "I wondered about that," he said. "I'm sorry--I should have--"

Jacob shook her head. "You're not my protector," she said. "I should have thought something like this would happen; it was *Freda's* portal, and Freda was a Healer. And she probably hoped someone would find Arlen--"

"She hoped a *Healer* would find him, because I touched her wrist before and nothing happened," Danny said. "Is she really dead?"

Jacob nodded. "I can't do anything for her," she said, and knelt next to the Hound's body. "If this is Kris, then there are two Hounds missing, unless there's another body somewhere."

"I don't smell any other bodies," Danny said, but he didn't sound very certain of himself. "But there's blood--Arlen's blood and someone else's blood, leading off thataway." He pointed into the forest, far past where Jacob could see, and kept pointing, his eyes widening. "Oh."

"What--" But even Jacob could see it; the faint outline of a tall building, familiar and yet, wrong in ways she couldn't quite pinpoint. "Of course. If you were a Hound and you were bound in the forest, where would *you* live?"

"But--" Danny shook his head. "This is too weird. If there are alternate Hounds and an alternate Darkbrook, is there an alternate *you?* Or me?"

"Espen said probably not," Jacob said.

"'Probably not' isn't exactly 'no'," Danny said.

"I don't think she knew for sure," Jacob admitted. "Do you think they'll let us in?" She stepped away from the bodies and tried not to shiver at the thought of finding both Hounds dead.

Danny stared at the dark bulk of Darkbrook and shook his head. "If those are the Hunt's wards, then which one is the wizard? Noah or Robin?"

Arlen's account had not included everything, and he hadn't been the best storyteller, which was almost to be expected. If Jacob's father had tried to kill her, she wouldn't have been very calm and collected either.

"My guess would be Noah," she said. "Arlen described him as being the youngest, and the Hunt did take students at first. At least in *our* world they did. Why would this one be any different?"

"And their Master is dead?" Danny asked, and shivered. "I'm glad. I don't think he would have had much use for a werewolf invading his territory."

"Probably not," Jacob agreed, and reached out to the wards that surrounded Darkbrook. "I don't feel anything from the wards."

"Are we really going in there?" Danny asked softly.

"How can I not?" Jacob asked, hoping that she sounded braver than she felt. "Someone--Nathaniel and Amalea, probably--will find Arlen, and he'll tell them what happened. And then Sennet will--"

"Will Sennet come if she knows a Healer had been murdered?" Danny asked the question that Jacob couldn't bring herself to voice.

"Sennet won't leave us here, and neither will my Uncle Lucas," Jacob said firmly. "And if one of those Hounds are wounded, I *can't* not help them."

Perhaps it was because she was a Healer, but she *felt* the binding now; a strangling hold around the entire forest that had been created in desperation and never revisited. Arlen hadn't said how long ago the Master of the Hunt had died, but perhaps it had been *his* influence that had prevented a surrender up until now.

"Can *we* leave?" Danny asked.

"The forest?" Jacob turned to stare at him. "Why wouldn't we be able to leave?"

"Because I don't smell any animals," Danny said, frowning. "No animals means no *food*."

"They're hiding," Jacob suggested. "Or they're--"

"How long has this Hunt been bound inside the forest?" Danny asked.

"A hundred years or so," Jacob said. "But--there *have* to be animals. It's a forest!" She glanced back at the bodies of Freda and Kris. Healer and Hound. "I feel like we should bury them."

"Birds, perhaps," Danny said, frowning. "But no deer. No rabbits. Maybe moles and mice and rats; it's hard to tell right here. But nothing else."

Jacob tried to imagine a hundred years of eating rats. Or worse. "Arlen didn't say that the Hounds were starving," she said. "But they have to be, don't they?"

"Someone was cooking meat over a fire not long ago," Danny said, "but that could have been the hunters and not the Hounds." He hesitated. "I'll help you bury the bodies later, but right now, shouldn't we find out if there are survivors?"

They walked, hand in hand, across the bridge that spanned the creek--no fish, Danny commented--and up to Darkbrook's front door without triggering the wards or any sort of alarm. But although their arrival had not triggered the wards, someone else had set a spell across the path, and Jacob stepped across it before she realized it was there.

"A human's spell," Danny said. "Perhaps it belongs to Arlen's uncle. He'll know we're here now. Or he'll know *someone* passed this way."

Jacob glanced around at the silent forest. "Do you think he could mask his scent from you?"

"He has no reason to believe I am anything but human," Danny said, keeping his voice low. "But the quicker we're inside Darkbrook, the better."

And they neither saw nor sensed anyone as they

approached the double doors. Danny pushed them open, and they both stepped inside.

Up until now, Jacob had relied on the moon and Danny's eyes to find her way through the forest. But inside, in utter darkness, she called up a light, and saw faint streaks of what had to be blood on the filthy floor, freshly dried.

"A few days old, at the most," Danny said when she pointed it out. "Arlen didn't say how long he was lying there--"

"I don't think he was conscious for a lot of it," Jacob said. "This is so strange. I'm used to Darkbrook being clean, and packed with students, not like this." Her voice echoed down the corridor. "Espen said there was a time lag between these two worlds, so it's hard to say how long Arlen was there before we came."

Danny made sure the door was shut behind them, then shook his head. "It does seem strange," he agreed. "This Darkbrook doesn't have quite the same layout as ours, does it?"

Walking carefully so as to not step in the blood, Jacob slowly made her way down the hall. "Not quite," she said after a moment as they emerged from the corridor into a small courtyard. "Although this would be nice to have, back home. And there's your meat."

Someone had been cooking the remains of a horse over a fire; the fire was gone now, the carcass only half cooked. What had interrupted the feast?

"What if they don't know we come in peace?" Danny asked, staring at what remained of the horse.

"The wards didn't try to keep us out, and no one has attacked us yet," Jacob pointed out. She realized she should probably feel frightened, but after Arlen's story, she *couldn't* feel scared. Perhaps some of Sennet's calm was starting to rub off on her after all.

"What should we do, then?" Danny asked. "Keep following the blood? Or wait?"

Jacob glanced up at the sky. The moon still shone in the sky, but there were hints of dawn around the edges of the trees now. She was just about to suggest they wait until the sun rose when the fire burst into flame behind them.

Danny shouted; Jacob jumped and threw up a ward that went nowhere, because the fire wasn't hellbent on attacking them at all. And in the confusion, a shadow detached itself from the wall behind them and stood beside the fire, quietly waiting until they noticed him.

Besides, the fire was behind them, and behind that, the exit. Jacob knew there had to be other ways out of this Darkbrook just like the other one, but *she* hadn't spent the last hundred years using this Darkbrook as her home. The Hound--a young man who resembled Josiah--had.

"We mean you no harm," Danny said quickly, as if he

expected the Hound to attack.

"I'm a Healer," Jacob said. "We found Freda's body--"

The Hound shuddered, and wiped one hand across his face. "If a Healer dies in the line of duty, the network of Healers will withdraw--"

"Not quite yet," Jacob said, hoping that was true. "Freda kept her portal open for a reason, and we spoke to Arlen."

"He lives?" The Hound's voice was only marginally more hopeful.

"He was alive when we left him, and there will be others trying to find us," Danny said.

"You are no Healer," the Hound said, frowning. He really *did* look like Josiah, only younger and less sure of himself. And much dirtier.

"No." Danny hesitated. "I'm a werewolf."

The Hound nodded. "You are lucky our Master is dead." He studied Jacob for a moment, and she noted the shadows under his eyes and the paleness of his skin under the dirt.

"Are you hurt?" she asked.

"No." His face crumpled, just enough for her to notice. "But Robin is."

"Robin is another Hound?" Danny asked.

"When Freda--the other Healer--took us to her portal, Arlen's uncle ambushed us," the Hound said. "He murdered Kris and Freda--he blames us for the Healer's death--and shot

Robin and Arlen. Robin still lives."

"What is your name?" Jacob asked. "I'm Jacob, and this is Danny."

The Hound took a step forward and swayed. "My name is Noah. But--even if you save him, they'll break through eventually. I can't hold them out forever. They've brought reinforcements."

Jacob felt something now, pulsing at the edges of the wards, an insidious worm of seeking, trying to find a crack in the Hound's defenses. Noah felt it, too--he reached out to grab hold of something and almost burned his hand in the fire.

"You're holding them back by *yourself?*" Danny asked as someone shouted outside.

"I have no choice," Noah whispered, and closed his eyes.

"Hound!" The voice came again, clearer now, as if the speaker was only a few feet away. "Surrender and your death will be quick!"

Without asking permission, Danny grabbed hold of Noah's arm and held him up. Noah tried to protest, to pull away, but he didn't have any strength to fight.

"Will you trust me with your wards?" Jacob asked softly.

Noah's eyes flew open. "Trust--*you?*"

Danny eased him down to the ground. "Arlen told us most of what happened," he said. "And right now, the hunters outside don't know we are here. Or they know *someone* is here, but not just us. Jacob, can you make wards strong enough to withstand that spell they're using?"

"I can do my best," Jacob said. "Noah? I need your permission."

Noah let out a breath in one great whoosh. "You have my permission." He made a motion with one hand and almost toppled over with the effort. "Our lives--are now in your hands."

There were tears on his cheeks; Jacob saw them glitter in the light of the fire. But she had no time for comfort; they were well-rested and well-fed and Noah was not. The hunters outside would know immediately that the Hounds were no longer alone, but that couldn't be helped.

Danny stayed near Noah, watching over him, but the Hound's head drooped and his eyes were closed by the time Jacob renewed the wards. She anchored them to the building, not herself, and found old remnants of the wards the Council had used back when this Darkbrook wasn't the home of the Hunt.

And the hunters outside could not get through. The sun had risen by the time she felt them withdraw.

"They--they leave at dawn and are back by dusk," Noah whispered, his eyes still closed. In sunlight, he seemed all the more exhausted; the grime on his skin only accentuating his pallor.

"Where is Robin?" Jacob asked. "How many days have passed since Freda died?"

Noah licked his lips. "Three?" He shook his head and forced his eyes to open. "I think three."

"Have you eaten?" Danny asked.

"I ate some of the horse," Noah said, but he didn't say how long ago that had been. In daylight, even Jacob could tell that the horse was beyond eating, but perhaps the Hounds didn't have the luxury of choosing fresh meat.

"Where is Robin?" she asked again.

Noah pointed at a door that led deeper into the main part of Darkbrook. "In there." But he made no move to rouse himself enough to show them the way. "In the library."

"Will you stay with him?" Jacob asked Danny. "He needs to rest."

"He needs to *eat*," Danny said, but didn't protest when she vanished through the door.

Finding Robin wasn't as hard as it seemed, since there was blood on the floor even here, and she found him lying senseless in the library, which was miraculously intact.

A cracked bowl of scummy broth held testament to Noah's attempts to feed the wounded Hound, but since the bowl was mostly full, Jacob doubted that Robin had eaten much at all. The wound from the crossbow bolt still seeped blood--the bandage was both sodden and filthy--but Noah had managed to pull out the bolt.

That had probably saved Robin's life.

As soon as Jacob's talent seeped under Robin's skin and began to repair the damage, he jerked awake, his eyes wide. He was in no shape at all to harm her, but she spoke to him quickly nonetheless, if only to soothe his fear.

"I am a Healer," she said. "Don't try to get up; you're badly wounded."

Robin pressed one hand against his stomach, and grabbed her hand with the other. "Perhaps--it might be best if you let me die."

"Noah has kept you alive this long," Jacob said. "I'd hate to disappoint him."

"We are prisoners?" Robin asked, and closed his eyes.

"No. You're still in Darkbrook." Quickly, before he lost consciousness or fell asleep, Jacob explained how she had come to be there. And for the longest time, she couldn't tell how much of the story he understood, because he didn't respond at all.

"Jacob?" Danny's voice came from the hallway, soft and low.

"In here," Jacob said, and glanced at him when he appeared. "Where's Noah?"

"He's asleep. I left him by the fire." Danny stopped behind Jacob. "Will he live?"

"He'll be fine, once he regains his strength," Jacob said. "But a day or two from now if I hadn't been here?" She shook her head.

"We would both be dead," Robin whispered, his eyes still closed.

"Yes, I think you would have been." Jacob did not stop him when he raised his hand to touch the scar that had once been a wound. "I can heal your wounds, but I can't give you back your strength. You need to rest."

"Noah--" Robin opened his eyes. "He brought me here?" He almost sounded surprised.

"Yes, he did," Danny said. "He told me what happened. He didn't cast his spell in time to save you--"

"Our Master would have left me to die," Robin whispered. He said this as a simple fact, nothing more, but Jacob felt some undercurrent of emotion beneath his words.

"Noah did not," she said, and wondered if Gabriel would have left his Hounds to die, once upon a time.

"And Kris is dead?"

"I'm sorry," Jacob said. "I couldn't help her. But Danny and I will help you bury her." Arlen had spoken of the graves in the courtyard, but she hadn't noticed them.

Robin nodded. "Thank you."

Jacob waited until he was asleep before standing and wiping her hands off on her jeans. "This isn't--"

"Don't say 'fair'," Danny said.

Jacob laughed. "I *was* going to say 'right'. This isn't right. Even if the Healers did bind the Hunt here, wouldn't they keep trying to create some sort of truce? And wouldn't they *notice* that the Hounds were being killed?"

"There are hundreds of worlds the Healers have to keep track of," Danny said diplomatically. "And there was a Healer here. Maybe they thought she would tell them if the Hounds' Master ever wanted a truce. Was his name Gabriel, too?"

"I don't know," Jacob said. "I don't think Arlen knew either." She walked over to the windows and stared out at the forest; so different but so much the same. "Do you think Nathaniel and Amalea have found Arlen yet?"

"If they have, then we won't have long to wait," Danny said. "But even if they haven't, can your wards withstand a day or two of this?"

"I'm not worried about my wards," Jacob said. And really, she wasn't. The spells the hunters had been using were powerful, but not powerful enough to break through wards that had been strong enough to help Jordan find a way to block his wild talent. "But I don't think the *Hounds* can wait until Sennet gets here."

Danny glanced down at Robin. "That horse isn't fit to eat anymore," he said. "And short of birds or bats--"

"There isn't any food here," Jacob said. "The hunters don't

realize it, but all they really have to do is wait them out. Eventually, they would try to escape."

"Why don't they try to escape?" Danny asked. "Why do the hunters just come at dawn and dusk?"

"Nothing can enter the forest *except* right around dawn and dusk," Noah said from the doorway. "There's a space of a couple hours between that makes it easier to enter--if you're not a Hound, of course."

He didn't look much better, but his eyes were a bit clearer.

"I suppose that had something to do with the fact that they didn't want anyone to just wander in?" Danny asked.

"It actually worked a bit in our favor, back where there were herds of deer around," Noah said. "But the deer have been gone for years now, and we--" He glanced down at Robin, bracing himself, Jacob thought, as if he expected to see him dead. "Is he--"

"He'll live," Jacob said. "You saved his life."

"What else could I have done?" Noah whispered, and closed his eyes.

It didn't seem like the type of question that needed an answer. "Does that mean we can't leave until dusk?"

"You are a Healer," Noah said, staring at her curiously. "You can come and go as you please."

"And anyone I might want to take with me?" Jacob asked.

"I don't know." Noah frowned. "That's an interesting

question." He sank down into a chair, trying to make it look like he hadn't almost collapsed into it, Jacob thought, and twisted his hands together. "The Healers used to come here--sometimes they came with other people, so I suppose you can do what you wish."

"Why did they come?" Danny asked.

Noah's mouth twisted. "They wanted us--the Hunt, our Master--to surrender. To submit to their binding, I suppose. But after a while, the Healers stopped coming. They left us alone for a long time."

"And then Arlen's uncle came?" Jacob asked.

"He said that since our Master refused to submit, he had been hired to kill us all," Noah said. "He said the Council had renewed itself, and that they wanted Darkbrook back."

"What did your Master say to that?" Danny asked.

Noah bowed his head. "He sent out six Hounds--only two came back. After that, it was war. But we really had no hope of winning."

"Is that horse your only source of food?" Jacob asked.

"It is not food anymore," Noah said. "I know that. But we have nothing else."

Danny rummaged in his pack and brought out a wrapped granola bar. He opened it and gave it to Noah, who stared at it warily.

"Eat it," Danny said. "It will help. It's not meat, but it's better than nothing."

"How many more of those do you have?" Jacob asked.

"Four," Danny said, and smiled at the expression on Noah's face when he bit into the granola bar. "You get used to the taste, after a while."

"Is there any water here?" Jacob asked. "At the very least, we can get Robin to *drink* something--"

"Outside," Noah said, still chewing. "In the creek."

"And they never thought to poison your water supply?" Danny asked.

Noah's face clouded. "Not yet."

"I'll go get some water," Danny offered. "I can smell the hunters if they're still here."

"Be careful," Jacob said. "Noah, there's *no* source of water inside?"

"Not that we've ever been able to find," Noah said. "I can go--"

"No," Jacob said quickly. "You stay here with Robin. Danny won't be long."

And Danny *wasn't* long at all. He returned in less than ten minutes with a jug full of water. "Are there spells to purify this, just in case?"

"Do you really think they'd poison the creek?" Jacob asked, and stared at the clear water in the jug. "I don't know if there are spells, but let me try this--" She sent her Healing talent into the water, and for the space of a heartbeat, it glowed a bright blue. And then, just as quickly, the glow was gone. "I don't know what that meant, but I think it's safe now, either way. Noah, do you want a drink?"

"There are cups," Noah said, and slid out of his chair to vanish down the hall. He returned a moment later bearing chipped mugs from Darkbrook's disused kitchens, dusty but clean enough for use.

Jacob gently woke Robin and managed to get him to drink half a cup before he fell asleep again. Noah drank his in small sips, savoring something as plain as water. Did it taste any different? Jacob couldn't tell, but she drank some anyway, and so did Danny.

She wasn't hungry--yet. But how long would it take for the wards to sap her strength? How many days?

When Noah fell asleep in his chair and Robin showed no sign of waking up, Jacob motioned Danny into the depths of the bookshelves. "What are we going to do? Four granola bars aren't going to last forever."

"I know," Danny said. "And the hunters will be back at dusk, and back again at dawn. There's no food here, and the only source of water is outside. Darkbrook wasn't built to withstand a siege."

"Did you smell any sign of the hunters?" Jacob asked.

"I smelled where they had been, but I didn't follow their

trail very far," Danny said. "And they might have done something to the water; they were at the very edge of the creek for a little while."

"I wonder if the Council really hired Arlen's uncle," Jacob said. "Arlen didn't mention them at all." She frowned, trying to think of a way to get the Hounds to safety without alerting the hunters. "Arlen said that Freda intended to bring the Hounds to a Healer's house--why didn't she take them to *her* house?"

"Maybe she knew they wouldn't be safe there," Danny said. "That would be the first place Arlen's uncle would look, I'd think, since the Healers created the binding."

Jacob shook her head. "If she had taken them to her house, she could have contacted Sennet through the mirror and let her know that they wanted to surrender. Arlen's uncle couldn't have pushed past a Healer's wards."

"Then perhaps she couldn't take them past the binding," Danny suggested. "She intended to use a portal to get them out of here--from *inside* the forest."

"That would mean we're stuck here," Jacob said. "I don't *want* to be stuck here." She chewed on her thumbnail for a moment, realized what she was doing, and shook her head. "Is there a *Veil* here?"

"It is closed against us, too," Noah said from the end of the set of bookshelves. "I appreciate your attempts to help us, but I'm not certain you can. Maybe it would be best--"

Jacob shook her head before he could finish. "No. You asked for the Healers to accept your surrender. Freda intended to take you to the other Healers so they could decide. I'm not about to do anything less than that, even if I'm not a full Healer yet." She hesitated, angry without quite knowing why. "I can't create a portal to get you out of here--"

Noah swallowed hard. "I can. Create a portal, I mean. But not out of here; within the boundaries of the forest."

"How will that help?" Danny asked. "I don't know very much about portals--"

"I know you can change their destinations," Jacob said. "If you know what you're doing, which I don't." She waved her arm to indicate the bursting bookshelves. "However, we have a library full of books that might be able to help."

"Is that how you learned how to create them?" Danny asked. "By reading these books?"

Noah hesitated, then nodded. "I was a student here, once," he said. "Before I was a Hound."

Jacob stared at him in shock. But why should she be shocked? It only made sense that the Hunt would have taken anyone, including students, back before the binding. For all she knew, Gabriel had done the same thing.

But to just *leave* them to suffer under the Master of this Hunt's wrath--

"What books did you use?" she asked.

"There's a whole section, over here," Noah said, and led them to the pertinent shelves. "Our Master wasn't--he wasn't interested in magic at first. But after he realized we were trapped here--" He pulled a book off the shelf, and Jacob noticed that his hands were shaking.

"Why don't you sit down?" she asked, keeping her voice gentle.

Danny fetched him a chair, and Noah sank down gratefully. After that, they gathered up all the books he could remember reading, and carried them over to the only table left in the room; a monstrosity of a library table that Jacob wasn't sure could have fit through the door.

For the next few hours as the sun shone outside, they read about portals. Noah tried to explain how they worked, but Jacob refused to let him cast one without resting first, and it didn't take him very long at all to fall asleep.

She took a nap while Danny kept watch, and then she kept watch over Danny while he did the same. And they shared one granola bar, careful to eat every crumb.

At dusk, the hunters returned. Jacob thought she felt them pass through the binding itself, but she definitely felt them when they arrived outside her wards.

Robin must have felt them, too, because he jerked awake with a gasp and whispered Noah's name.

"He's asleep," Jacob said. "How do you feel? We have

water, and you can have a granola bar if you're hungry." And then, as he stared at her, she added, "I have the wards." She'd cast a spell-light, too, dimmed against any sign of detection from outside.

"You--you told me who you were," Robin said slowly. He glanced at Danny, stiffened, and tried to rise. "I can't--I can't remember."

"You were badly wounded," Jacob said. "I'm a Healer, and Danny's with me. My name is Jacob." She told him the story of their arrival, and what had happened since then.

"The hunters are back," Robin said, and glanced at Danny again. "You're--"

"I'm a werewolf," Danny said.

"Of course you are," Robin said, and Jacob thought he looked a bit relieved.

"What happens if you try to go through the Veil?" Danny asked.

Robin slowly sat up, using the wall for balance. "We die," he said. "The elves have long memories."

"So our only other option is a portal," Jacob said. "Noah said he could--"

"He shouldn't--" Robin took a deep breath. "I'm sorry. I didn't mean to interrupt."

"I don't think he's strong enough to form a portal," Jacob said quietly.

"He's not," Robin said. "He sent Arlen away with one, and it took him *hours* to wake up after that. We tried--" he hesitated. "We tried to find food for him and keep him safe, because he kept *us* safe. But--"

"How old was he when he was made into a Hound?" Danny asked.

Robin shook his head. "I don't know. We were never told such things."

"Thirteen," Noah said from his spot near the wall. He yawned and stretched, and glanced out the window. Only then did he realize what time it was. "You--you really *do* have my wards. I can't feel the hunters outside. Are they there?"

"There are five of them standing on the other side of the creek," Jacob said. "At the moment, they're not trying to get inside. They're just standing there, trying to figure out my wards."

"Robin, do you want some water to drink? Or a granola bar?" Danny offered both, and Robin took the granola bar dubiously, glancing to Noah for help.

"It's like--cereal," Noah said, but that didn't seem to help. "It's food. It will help. Eat it."

Robin took a bite, made a face, and chewed silently, washing down the remnants with some of the water. "You saved my life," he said, once he had finished eating.

Noah crossed his arms. "I told you. We have to stick

together." He glanced at Jacob and Danny, then noticed the books piled on the table. "I could show you--"

"Actually, I think I might have figured it out," Danny said. "And Jacob wants to try to cast one before we make you do it, okay?"

Jacob hadn't said anything of the sort, but Noah didn't need to know that. And even then, if she *did* manage to cast a portal, where would she have it lead? She couldn't cast a portal directly to Sennet's house unless she stood in a Healer's house already, and she had no idea how to find Freda's house in the first place. If she cast a portal to the forest like Freda had, and the Wild Hunt showed up, what would happen to *her* Hounds?

And how much more difficult would it be to create a portal that led to another *world,* much less another spot in the forest while holding onto the wards she had taken from Noah?

"We'll be right back," Jacob said. "I want to try it out in the hallway, just in case." Just in case she embarrassed herself in front of the Hounds.

Noah looked like he wanted to protest, but he held his tongue after he glanced at Robin. "Be careful, then," he said.

Jacob nodded and followed Danny out into the hallway.

In theory, portals weren't difficult to create. Doorways worked best, because they already led to a different place. The wild portals that appeared in the forest back home usually found a home in the natural arches between two trees, or where a branch had broken. But that wasn't the *only* way to create them. Some people could create portals out of mirrors, or reflective surfaces, like a still pool of water.

Jacob closed a door on the opposite end of the hallway. "Do you want to try first?"

"You can't just create a portal leading to anywhere," Danny said. "Where should we try?"

"I think we should try somewhere inside Darkbrook first," Jacob said. "Like the courtyard. If that works, then we'll try somewhere else." All of the books had claimed that you could only create portals to lead to places you had already seen. That left out almost everywhere in *this* world, and Jacob had no idea how difficult it would be to create a portal back home. But she was willing to try.

"I think that's a good idea," Danny said. "Do you want to go first?"

Jacob placed her hand on the door and closed her eyes. When she spoke the spell, she felt something shimmer through her connection with the door, and when she opened it, instead of the room beyond, she saw the courtyard, dark and quiet in the moonlight.

The fire had died down; only a few coals remained.

Jacob stepped through her portal, and Danny followed. On the opposite side, they found another door--the portal had *not* come out through a door, which was interesting--and

Danny tried the same spell. This time, nothing happened.

"Werewolves have never been very good at magic," Danny said.

"Well, let me try again," Jacob said. She spoke the spell again, her hand pressed against the open door, but this time, something felt different. Less--less in her control. When she opened the door, she didn't see the hallway leading to the library where they had left the Hounds. Instead, she saw an opulent room filled with books--*another* library--and two elves, one sitting behind a polished desk, the other standing in front of what had to be a mirror.

"...keep me out," the standing elf said, oblivious to the fact that the portal was live. "I don't care *who* created the binding--"

The other elf stood up, pushing back her chair so quickly that it fell on the floor. "Wait! Don't close--"

Jacob slammed the door shut.

"What was *that?*" Danny asked, stepping back away from the door.

"I don't know," Jacob admitted. "But it felt different this time, when I spoke the spell. Can someone take *control* of your portal from the other end?"

"The books didn't say anything about that," Danny said, "but--maybe we should *walk* back to the library. Noah might know."

Jacob studied the door for a moment, then opened it. It

opened onto a hallway this time, still in Darkbrook, perfectly mundane.

"The other elf didn't want us to close the door," she said. "Or that's what I *think* she started to say--and Amalea's an elf--"

"If they were looking for us, they know we're here now," Danny replied.

"And they know we're in Darkbrook, alive and unharmed." Jacob frowned. "But they *don't* know about the Hounds." She felt something change outside; a subtle shift in the wards and the binding that told her the hunters' window of attack was swiftly closing. And as they had at dawn, the group of hunters started to move away. But were there still five? Jacob couldn't tell.

"We'll need more water," Jacob said. "Or else I can try to cleanse the entire creek."

"Why the entire creek?" Danny asked.

"Because right now, the Hounds look like refugees from a war," Jacob said. "They're starving to death and they're frightened. Even if there's no meat for them to eat here, there should be plenty of wild food in the forest. We just have to find it for them. The library should have books on harvesting wild food."

"So we feed them, find them clothes--then what?"

"If the elves were looking for us, they're not going to stay away for long," Jacob said, trying to come up with a plan. "At dawn, the hunters will return, and there might be elves with them."

"The elves can probably come and go as they please," Danny said.

"Then in that case, they might come earlier," Jacob replied. "And the Hounds can't *look* like Hounds if they come. They have to look more civilized. More like us and less likely to attack at any provocation."

"They don't look very likely to attack right now," Danny said as they rounded the corner that led to the library. "I think--"

"Something happened," Noah said from the doorway. "I felt it. You vanished, and then you tried to come back, but something happened."

Jacob explained what had happened as soon as Robin was in listening distance. "We're not really supposed to be here," she said. "There are probably people looking for us."

"Elves?" Noah asked. "Why would the *elves* look for you?"

Jacob hesitated. "You know we're not from here," she said. "We're not from this *world*. In our world, the Wild Hunt--"

"There are *two*--" Robin's eyes narrowed. "Two Hunts? How?"

"In our world, the Hunt was bound by the Council," Danny said.

Noah made a swift motion with one hand, not to cast any spells, but as if he wanted to wipe away Danny's words. Neither Hound looked very happy, and Jacob didn't blame them. They were under siege, after all; tired and hungry and this wasn't helping anything at all.

"You trusted me with your wards," she said. "Will you trust me with this, too?"

"We have no choice," Noah said, and sat down against the wall. "You are not supposed to be here, but yet you are here, and you--" He closed his eyes. "Let us say there is another Hunt. As we were not bound by the Council, they were."

"A hundred years have passed," Jacob said. "The Hunt is now free from the Council's binding, and live as a family in Faerie. Their Master isn't as frightening as he used to be."

"Our Master would still be frightening," Robin said. "Though you would not have lived to meet him." He nodded to Danny. "Especially you. We...you realize we had no *choice* about what he had us do? We could not protest or fight against him. He *owned* us."

"The elves that you saw--their Veil reaches past your binding," Noah said. "I've been to the edge before. Do you think--you could make a portal back to the room you saw, and we could--" He drew in a breath and almost choked on it. "Perhaps they would see that we mean them no harm." But a tear leaked down his cheek when he closed his eyes, and he did not sound as if he believed his own words.

"The other Hunt--have they redeemed themselves?" Robin's voice cracked.

"I'm not sure *they* believe they have, but other people think they have," Jacob said softly. "Are you sure you want me to open another portal? What if they're waiting on the other side with weapons to kill you?"

"Can you open a portal and not allow anyone to cross through at first?" Noah asked. "A portal with a ward?"

"I can try," Jacob said doubtfully, "but I'm not sure it will work."

"Try," Noah said. "Please."

Robin's eyes were closed, his face still. But he nodded at Noah's words. "Please. I'm tired."

"I'm tired of fighting," Noah whispered. "I'm tired of all of this. I just want--if I am allowed to want *anything,* all I want is for this to be over. And short of dropping the wards and allowing the hunters inside--" He bowed his head. "I would rather die by the elves, I think."

"I would rather you not die," Jacob said, close to tears. "I--" She glanced at Danny. "Danny?"

"I don't think you need to die to end this," Danny said softly. "But if the Veil intersects the binding, which one is more powerful?"

Noah's eyes snapped open. He stared at Danny, the

weariness gone; the light back in his gaze. "I...I don't know." He glanced at Robin, whose eyes were still closed. "None of us have ever made it past the Veil, as far as I know."

"Why don't we find out?" Jacob asked. "We can use this door right here--" She closed it, then glanced at Danny and Noah for approval. Both nodded. Noah scrambled up and pressed himself against the wall; Danny stood beside her where he'd been before.

It wasn't difficult at all to anchor the portal to the elves' library. Jacob remembered the room quite well, even though she'd only seen it for an instant. It was the type of room that you couldn't easily forget. The shelves of books; a fire in the fireplace. The desk, all polished and gleaming. Perhaps the elves' portal had come through a mirror; that *would* make sense, in a way.

When Jacob opened the door with her wards in place, the girl no longer sat at the desk, but the other elf--the one who hadn't noticed the portal's opening, was standing near the back of the room, his back to them, furiously paging through a thick book and muttering to himself.

It sounded like he was complaining about something, but Jacob couldn't make out his words.

"Can he *hear*--" Noah began, and the elf turned around.

"Wait--please," he said quickly, as if he was afraid Jacob would close the portal again. *"Don't shut the door."*

"I won't," Jacob said, and crossed her arms, standing straight in front of the portal so it would be hard for him to see behind her. "Not unless you give me cause to close it."

"We gave you no cause before," the elf said. "May I have your name? Mine is Camren."

"Jacob," Jacob said. "Jacob Lane. I'm a--"

"A Healer, yes, we know," Camren said. "My sister received notice from our distant cousin Amalea that you might be here. Is your--companion--"

"Danny," Danny said, stepping up beside Jacob. "And we're fine. *Unharmed.*"

"But you're in *Darkbrook,*" the elf protested. "I recognize that room--"

"Is the Veil stronger than the binding?" Jacob asked.

Camren blinked. "Of course it is. But you're not bound by the binding. You're a Healer. And your--Danny--isn't bound by it either."

"But we are," Noah said from the shadows behind them.

"You--" Camren squinted, trying to see into the shadows. "And you are--?"

"Who *else* would they be?" Jacob asked. "This is *Darkbrook,* as you said."

"Impossible," Camren stated. "The Hunt is a wild thing. They cannot be reasoned with. They *have* no reason, other than to murder anyone who stands in their way."

"Simon Parker killed our Master eight months ago," Noah said softly. "He has not declared this yet because he does not know."

Camren's mouth fell open and he stood there, clutching his book to his chest, staring. And then he shook himself, carefully placed the book on top of the desk, and stood there for a moment, staring down at it.

"I see." Jacob barely heard him speak. He glanced up. "I must fetch my sister. Will you stay?"

"I'm holding the wards against the hunters *and* this portal," Jacob warned. "I don't know how long I can hold both."

Camren nodded. "Fair enough. If you have to leave, will you come back, then?"

"Yes," Jacob said. "I'll open the portal again."

"I will be as quick as I can," Camren promised, and almost ran out the door.

"How long should I leave it open?" Jacob asked, turning to face the Hounds.

"Not long," Noah said. "I--I never left them open for very long at all. I didn't trust the hunters not to find a way through." He stepped up to the portal and stared into the elves' library. Jacob wondered what he thought about what he saw.

"Have you read all of the books in this library?" she asked instead.

Noah glanced back at the dark and dusty shelves. "Yes."

And he wasn't boasting, just stating a fact. "When our Master died, I had to--I had to find a way to keep the wards in place and I had to try to keep the other Hounds alive. I failed."

"No." Robin sounded tired. "No, you did the best you could under the circumstances. You couldn't do any more than you did."

Noah shrugged, as if he disagreed but didn't want to start an argument. "I could have done more," he said.

Before Robin could reply to that, the door opened again, and the girl Jacob and Danny had seen walked into the room, closely followed by Camren.

Noah didn't fade into the shadows quickly enough; the girl spotted him immediately, and held out her hand. "Please don't disappear. You are a Hound?"

"Yes." Noah stared at her, both solemn and wary. "Yes, I am."

"Camren says your Master is dead," the girl said. "Simon Parker has not declared that; you were right in thinking that he does not know for certain."

Noah cocked his head. "Camren also says that Hounds are--"

"Perhaps I spoke in error," Camren said quickly, "because I did not know the truth. I apologize. It is quite obvious now that Hounds are rational beings."

"It was our Master who was not," Robin said from the

shadows.

Camren's lips twitched. "Yes, I believe we can agree with that."

"May I ask--" the girl hesitated. "I have not introduced myself, have I? My name is Bernadette. You know my brother Camren. Did you give him your names?"

"That's a very human name," Danny said when no one spoke.

Bernadette smiled. "Our mother was fond of human names. You must be Daniel. And Jacob Lane--Amalea gave us a good description of you both."

"My name is Noah," Noah said, and glanced back at Robin. "Robin."

The two elves waited a beat, as if they expected more, and Jacob realized that they truly didn't know how many Hounds Arlen's uncle had killed.

And then, before she could speak, Camren ventured, "There are only *two* of you?"

"Less than a week ago, there were four of us left," Robin said. "And three days ago, there were three of us left."

"Does he *know*?" Bernadette asked faintly. "Does Simon Parker *know* there are only two of you left?"

"I think he knows now," Noah said. "Or again, he suspects. But we cannot negotiate with him. He will not stop until we are all dead." He said this with a quiet intensity the elves could not miss.

"Negotiate?" This from Camren. "I'd say--"

"We captured Arlen three--maybe four days ago--and we asked him to give a message to the Healer Freda. We wanted to negotiate our surrender," Noah said. "But before she could take us to the other Healers, Arlen's uncle killed her."

"Technically, Arlen is missing," Bernadette said. "Camren and I know he is safe, but we haven't spoken to him. And his uncle claims that *you* were responsible for the Healer's death."

"He *would* claim that," Jacob said. "But Danny and I have spoke to Arlen, and his uncle was responsible. *And* Arlen almost died because of this."

"You are a Healer," Camren said. "Can't *you* accept their surrender and be done with the binding?"

"I'm only fourteen years old," Jacob said, struggling to keep her voice civil. "And I'm not a member of the Healer network yet. This is the second portal I've made in my entire life, and I have idea how to get back home. If Arlen's uncle has killed one Healer already, what will stop him from murdering me *and* the Hounds? *And* Danny?"

Something passed in front of the wards outside, but it was gone too quickly for Jacob to identify it. Had one of the hunters *stayed?* She frowned, listening, but the presence did not return, and she felt nothing through the binding itself.

"You are not safe in Darkbrook," Bernadette stated.

"None of you are. If what you say is truth, then Simon Parker *won't* stop until all of the Hounds are dead. And perhaps he has become a twin to the Master of the Hunt, because he lusts for their blood now, long after this could have ended."

"We would surrender to you in exchange for our lives," Noah whispered.

"Yes, I expect you would," Camren said. "But what would *we* do with you? There are those who would agree that the Hunt should be wiped from existence. There are those who would not hesitate to kill you, even here. If we held you prisoner, then what have you traded? Free run of an entire forest for a cell?" He shook his head. "No. We'll not accept your surrender."

Noah's face froze, then crumpled, just enough for Jacob--and probably the elves--to notice. "But we will *die* if you--"

"'The Hunt is a wild thing. They cannot be reasoned with. They *have* no reason, other than to murder anyone who stands in their way.'" Bernadette quoted her brother even though she had not been in the room when he had spoken. "Have I covered all of it?"

"You forgot the part where the Hunt is evil incarnate," Robin said, appearing from the shadows, his face set and still. "Or the part in which we murder babies in their cribs, or steal children from their beds. Or was that the elves? I think the stories got mixed up a bit here and there."

"No doubt they did," Camren said. "That, too, then. But rest assured, the Hunt *cannot* be reasoned with."

"What do you mean?" Noah asked, confused. He wasn't the only one who was confused, although Jacob thought that Danny knew exactly where the elves were going with this.

"I see no Hounds here," Bernadette said firmly. "I see two *people* who--under terrible circumstances--were forced to do terrible things, once upon a time. And it wouldn't be unreasonable at all to assume that you both have been doing your best just to stay alive with no one to help you or no one to care whether you lived or not. Am I right?"

Noah glanced at Robin, then back at the elves. "But we--we *are* Hounds."

"Does the Hunt still exist?" Camren asked gently. "Without a Master?"

"Of course it wouldn't," Jacob said when Noah didn't speak. "The Hunt needs a Master to exist. Doesn't it?"

"Yes, but--" Noah frowned at Bernadette. "You are saying that since our Master is dead, the Hunt is no more, and we are--"

"Well, you *should* be free to go," Bernadette said. "But the Healers will make that decision. I have my doubts they will attempt to imprison you or harm you in any way."

"And Simon Parker?" This from Robin, who had crossed

his arms in front of his chest, as if to brace himself against bad news.

"We will see about Simon Parker," Camren said, and his smile held more than a bit of fury.

"And even though we are Hounds--" Noah was still struggling with the elves' definitions.

It *was* a neat little solution, Jacob thought. Of *course* the Hunt could not exist without a Master. Of *course* the Hounds had been forced to do terrible things on their Master's orders; things they could not refuse to do. Noah had once been a student at Darkbrook; Jacob knew full well that he had never asked to be a Hound. She wasn't sure about Robin's origins, but the odds were also on his side.

"I would welcome you all to our home," Bernadette said. "Jacob, you'll have to release your wards for you all to be able to come through the portal."

"I thought I felt something outside the wards," Jacob said doubtfully. "Are you sure I have to release them?"

"That's the only way," Camren said. "We can't come through, and *you* can't come through without releasing them. But once you're here, Simon Parker cannot even hope to find you."

"Release them," Noah said hoarsely.

"But how do we know we can trust you?" Danny asked softly. "How do we know you're not in league with the hunters?"

Noah stiffened, and turned towards him. "Do we have a *choice?*"

Bernadette hesitated. "I had intended to wait until you arrived to tell you this, Daniel, but--wait a moment, please." Before Danny could respond, she left the room, leaving Camren behind.

"I don't blame you for your suspicion," he said easily. "I would be suspicious too. But--truthfully, when an elf gives his word, he--or she--is bound by it. And I would go so far as to assure your safety here. *All* of you."

Bernadette returned with a blonde haired woman who held a little girl in her arms. Jacob didn't recognize her, but Danny obviously did; he stared, open-mouthed, shocked into stillness.

"Amalea told us that she intended to tell you where your family was; she had known since you returned that they were here and safe. But she wasn't certain of her reception, so she didn't speak of it to you." Bernadette's voice softened at the expression on Danny's face. "She said there are only a few places that would be obvious locations for your family to be exiled; we found them for her, and had intended to let her know when you both disappeared."

"Mother?" Danny's voice cracked. "This could still be some sort of a trick--"

Danny's mother sighed. "I commend your caution," she

said, "but I have never once in my life--" The little girl squirmed out of her arms. "This is your sister Yasmin. And I am very happy to see you well, my son."

The little girl approached the portal timidly, staring up at Danny with wide eyes. His mother fumbled in her pocket for something, then held out a flat medallion, well-worn and almost unreadable. "This belonged to your father and to his father as well. You were wearing it the night you died, and I found it that next morning. No one can read the inscription anymore, but I know what it says and I think you know, too. I don't think an imposter would be able to tell you that it reads--"

She said something then, in another language Jacob didn't know.

Danny let out a breath. "Okay, I'm convinced. I'm...I'm more than convinced. I have a lot of apologies to make, Mother, and I--"

Danny's mother smiled. "We can talk more when you get here," she said. "And now, if you don't mind, Jacob, will you release your wards so I can see my son again?"

Jacob cast one last net for the presence outside and found nothing again. She glanced back at Robin and Noah, then released the wards in one swift motion, leaving Darkbrook exposed to any attack.

When she turned back to the portal, she heard Danny gasp,

and on the other side, Camren make some sort of protest before he was cut off by a voice Jacob recognized even though she knew she'd never heard it before.

"Do you think the elves are the only ones able to hijack portals?" Arlen's uncle asked, and stepped into the room. He held a crossbow in his hands, loaded and ready to fire. "Now. All of you. Back up against the wall." When no one moved, he shot one bolt into a bookcase, perilously close to Danny's head. "Move!"

"You don't want to do this," Jacob said, trying to get him to listen to reason. "The elves--"

Arlen's uncle curled his lip and spat on the floor. "Have the *elves* ever helped us rid the forest of the Hunt? Did the *elves* hasten to our aid when the Hunt was murdering everyone in its path?" He motioned with his crossbow. "Line up against the wall or I'll shoot you where you stand."

Jacob took one step backwards, the spell for the wards still fresh in her mind and ready to be spoken. But could she speak it before he shot one of the Hounds? Or, perhaps a *different* set of wards could save them--

With an angry gesture, Arlen's uncle dismissed the portal. Jacob felt nothing; no sign that it had ever been hers. He must have waited outside the wards; perhaps he felt her first portal open and knew she was not a Hound.

"Back up," he growled, and aimed the crossbow at Danny,

who--suddenly-- wasn't there.

Werewolves weren't very good at magic. They were good at wards, yes, and they were very, very hard to kill. In the blink of an eye, Danny had shifted into his wolf form, showing Arlen's uncle just what he was up against.

Growling, he ignored the order and advanced.

"Are your crossbow bolts silver?" Jacob asked, her voice shaking. "Because I have it on good faith that the only way to kill a werewolf is with a silver--"

Danny lunged. The shot went wild, and for a very long moment, Jacob thought that he would end it; that he would kill Arlen's uncle just as easily as she could heal the wounded.

But the third bolt in the crossbow had a wad of something wrapped around its tip. With a howl of fury, Arlen's uncle lit the tip and cast a spell--Jacob was too busy concentrating on the wards she'd placed around herself and the Hounds to hear it--and shot the last bolt into the nearest bookshelf, which burst into flames.

"No!" Noah started forward and Arlen's uncle pulled out a gun.

"*I* have it on good faith that Hounds die just as easily as anyone else," Arlen's uncle said. "And while the bullets in this gun might not *kill* a werewolf, a shot through his brain would slow him down enough for me to take care of the rest of you. *Call off your wolf!*"

"You want us, not them," Robin said, and positioned himself in front of Noah. "Let them go. They are not involved in this."

"Didn't I kill you once before?" Arlen's uncle asked, his voice cold. He fired the gun, not at Danny, but at Robin.

Wards were no match for gunfire. Robin fell back, still protecting Noah, but Noah hadn't been idle. With a shout, he threw out his hand and the door slammed shut behind Arlen's uncle, rattling in its frame. Danny leaped--Arlen's uncle fired the gun again and Jacob screamed as something whipped past her head.

Thick smoke obscured the room now, but Jacob thought she heard glass breaking somewhere; she dropped to her knees to get out of the worst of it and heard the gun fire again.

How many bullets did he have left? She knew nothing about guns.

She ended up beside Robin, who lay sprawled against the wall, his eyes closed but the wound in his arm not life-threatening at all. But there was glass in his hair and a lump on the back of his head; evidently he'd hit his head on his way down.

And then, amazingly, it started to rain. Indoors. That had to be Noah's doing; Jacob couldn't imagine why Arlen's uncle would want to put out the fire, but she still couldn't see the other Hound *or* Danny. Arlen's uncle couldn't see them either, but it wouldn't take him long to spot Jacob and Robin.

The rain let up as soon as the fire was out, but smoke still hung heavily in the air. Arlen's uncle took a step towards the bookshelves and slid a little, which gave Jacob an idea to end this--she reached out her hand to the nearest puddle of water and whispered the spell to freeze it.

The second step Arlen's uncle took was on pure, slick ice, already starting to melt in the hot air. He tried to catch his balance, saw Jacob sitting beside Robin, and leveled his gun at her right before he fell.

The gun never fired. When Jacob dared to open her eyes, she saw Danny standing over Arlen's uncle, the gun in *his* hand, and Noah beside him covered in soot.

The door opened. Arlen's uncle tried to rise, but the ice was still slick and when he saw that Danny held his gun, he froze on the floor, the fury on his face frightening to see.

Behind the door, not *quite* an army of elves, but enough of them to cause Noah to back away and almost fall himself.

The tableau must have been strange enough to give them pause, because they hesitated as they entered the room, and Arlen's uncle must have thought to try one more time to bend the truth to his own gain.

"How ever did you *find* me?" he asked, and held out his hand for the nearest elf to help him up. "I've been trying to--"

"Quiet," the elf snapped, not taking the bait. "Um, Jacob

Lane?"

"Can you arrest him?" Jacob asked. "Because he has already murdered one Healer, not to mention--"

Robin groaned beside her and opened his eyes.

"How many Hounds did he kill after your Master died?" Jacob asked.

"Fourteen," Robin whispered, staring at Arlen's uncle. "Fourteen."

"Fourteen Hounds who were only in the wrong place at the wrong time," Jacob said. "And I'm sure there have been others."

"He murdered a *Healer?*" the elf who had spoken asked, almost disbelieving. "But if you murder a Healer--"

"That's out of my hands," Jacob said firmly, and stood up.

Danny handed the gun over to one of the elves, who tucked it into the waistband of his breeches and nodded his thanks.

"Our lord and lady Camren and Bernadette request your presence," the elf who had spoken said. "All of you, except for *him*." He nudged Arlen's uncle with the toe of his boot.

"I have acted under the authority of the Council," Arlen's uncle protested, and tried to rise again. He made it halfway up this time before he noticed the sword at his throat, and the other swords around him, just waiting for an excuse to finish him off.

But the elves did not finish him off. They pulled him up instead, and marched him to the portal, not slipping or sliding on the ice at all even though Arlen's uncle could barely keep his balance without them. He cursed the Hounds, then, and threw some sort of a spell that fizzled halfway to where Robin still sat against the wall.

"Your lord and *lady*?" he repeated.

The elf smiled. "Yes. Will you come?"

Noah took that moment to collapse; the strain of the portal had stolen all his strength. Danny caught him before he could fall, and as the elves tried to help, a familiar face appeared in the doorway.

"You!" Robin's voice cracked.

Espen smiled. "You recognize me? Good. This might not be as difficult as I thought it would be."

"You've come here before," Noah whispered from where Danny had lowered him to a chair. "You...you asked--"

"Someone take control of this portal," Espen snapped. "I don't care who, but do it, *please.*"

A moment later as one of the elves took the portal from Noah's control, the Hound's face regained some of its color. "It is your binding, milady, that makes it so difficult."

"About the binding," Espen said. "You intend to go into Faerie, and the Veil *is* more powerful than the binding. However, what did you intend to do once you arrived?"

"Seek you out and negotiate our surrender," Noah said. "We said the same to Freda before he--before Simon Parker murdered her."

"We would have known if you were guilty either way," Espen said. "So be assured he would not have held the lie as truth for long."

The elves were gone now, except for the one who had spoken. But there were other people on the other side of the portal, waiting; Jacob spotted Danny's mother and a host of like-featured family, and she thought she saw Bernadette, too.

"Danny, your family is waiting for you," she said.

Danny nodded. "I'm not going anywhere until this is over."

Espen raised an eyebrow at him. Since Jacob had been on the receiving end of that look, she knew exactly what to expect, but Danny seemed a bit at a loss.

"I don't know who you are," he said. "And I didn't risk my life to leave Noah and Robin alone in the end."

"As you were not left alone in the end," Espen said. "I am a Healer, like Sennet, like your Gen, like Jacob. Some would assume that I am the Healer's leader, for want of a better word, but there are no leaders in the Healer's network."

She had their attention now; even the elf forgot himself long enough to stare.

"We tried to negotiate a binding with the Master of the Hunt here," Espen said. "We failed. We tried to kidnap

Hounds to free them. Again, we failed. Those we 'rescued' were still under their Master's influence, and they killed themselves, each and every time."

Noah flinched. Perhaps he had known some of those Hounds.

"We knew there were innocents in the Hunt; those who did not wish to be Hounds, but what could we do? Short of finding a way to murder the Master of the Hunt--and Healers *do not* kill, we had no choice but to bind them inside the forest." Espen stared at Robin, who hadn't moved. "This stopped the killing."

"But it *didn't* stop the killing," Jacob said, daring to argue with her. "Arlen's uncle--"

"If the Council has truly reconvened, they are much reduced from their previous size. We'll be talking with them later on if we can find them; they had no authority to do this, and they did *not* ask our permission to attempt to win back the forest and Darkbrook from the Hunt. I have no way of knowing if Freda knew what was happening in the forest--"

"She knew," Robin whispered. "She asked us if our Master would have negotiated a surrender."

"He wouldn't have," Noah said.

"But once your Master was dead, someone should have told the Healers," Espen said, as if that would have prevented the rest of the deaths.

"Who?" Jacob asked. "The only person they had seen for years was Arlen's uncle, and he was bent on killing them all. How could they contact the Healers? How many times did Arlen go with his uncle to hunt?"

"Just that one time," Noah said. "He wasn't with the others any other time. I saw he wasn't an adult and thought he would be easier to capture." He straightened up in his chair as he spoke, but his voice was still shaky. "Robin caught him--"

"If you intended to have a way for us to contact someone on the outside if our Master were to die and we wanted to surrender, then you should have put something into place," Robin said. "But we had no other recourse."

For a moment, Espen seemed angry, as if she wanted to protest that the Healers had done no wrong. But then she nodded, and sighed, and some of the terrible power that made everyone so afraid of her drained out of her bearing.

"You are right," she said. "We should have thought towards that possibility, and we did not. Perhaps if we had placed some sort of spell around Darkbrook, or--"

"It doesn't matter now," Noah said. "What matters now is what will happen to us next. Whether or not you will accept our surrender."

"As Bernadette so nicely put it, the Hunt is gone. It no longer exists. You may be Hounds, but you cannot be a Hunt without a Master, and I would suggest that you don't go searching for one just yet. You've done quite well on your own. The binding kept the Hunt in captivity, not individual Hounds."

"That doesn't answer the question of what will happen to them next," Danny said shortly.

"I don't believe that's up to me," Espen said. "It is up to Noah and Robin. Although since memories are rather long around here, I'd suggest that you start anew, somewhere else."

Jacob folded her arms. "Like where? You're not just going to leave them somewhere and expect them to be able to live--"

"Oh, no," Espen said. "They'll definitely need help. And friends. And perhaps--eventually--a family." She was staring at Jacob as she spoke, and Jacob wondered if Espen was thinking of the Wild Hunt; the *other* Wild Hunt, the success story instead of the failure. "In these instances, a Healer is usually asked to take charge of the well-being of those involved. You're rather young, Jacob, but since you're involved in this already--"

"They can come back with us?" Jacob asked. "Both of them? Together?"

"Wait a minute," Robin said. "There's another *Hunt* where you live--you told us that yourself--" He stared at Espen. "You're just going to let us *go*?"

"Brenna is a Hound, and she's not a member of the Wild Hunt," Espen said. "And she's doing better now that she's around other children her own apparent age."

That was true. Jacob hadn't heard the whole of Brenna's story, but she'd been at Darkbrook for almost year now, and the person who had kept her a hound for a hundred years had been dead for just about the same amount of time.

"Even so," Robin said, still unconvinced.

"Give me a reason not to let you go," Espen suggested. "And don't say because you are Hounds; that particular issue has been resolved."

Noah opened his mouth, then closed it again. Robin glanced at him, frowned, and shook his head, his eyes bright with tears.

"Then let us leave this place," Espen said. "I assure you we will treat the graves with the dignity they deserve; those who died here will *not* be forgotten."

Together, with Espen leading, they walked single-file through the portal, and left the dusty halls of Darkbrook behind.

Chapter Five

T wo days passed in relative quiet. The Hounds slept and ate and slept again; Jacob kept watch over their beds as the elves ran to and fro to keep them comfortable.

Danny's family was a riot of good cheer; his mother and brothers and sisters and in some cases, *their* children--all together in a mass of wolves and humans, joyous at his return.

She saw Espen here and there, and Bernadette and Camren, and heard rumors of something not quite right in the story of things, but she didn't really think there could be something *wrong* until she went to visit the Hounds and found them gone.

Jacob only had a moment of panic before she thought to ask a passing elf and found her way to the kitchens. She found them with Camren in a room that was a far cry from the kitchens at Darkbrook, sitting at a wooden table that would have been at home in any mundane kitchen.

At first, no one noticed her in the bustle of activity around the two Hounds. That the cooks were elves and not human, only meant that the use of magic was not banned from these kitchens.

Both Noah and Robin seemed a bit lost, silent and wary, their eyes wide as they watched the elves at work. And the mountain of food in front of them only grew and grew.

"Eat," Camren suggested. "There are others gathering you both some additional clothing, but we thought you must be hungry."

They wore hand-me-downs from the elves, and someone had washed most of the dirt from their skin, but Jacob didn't think they'd been introduced to the actual baths yet, which were wonderful things.

"We can't eat all of this," Noah said, and the bustle stilled, the elves all waiting for Camren's reply.

Robin hunched his shoulders, well-aware of the elves' regard.

"It's no matter," Camren said. "Eat what you can. Someone else will eat the rest."

That seemed to satisfy them; but they only really relaxed when most of the elves disappeared with varying excuses, and Jacob had to wonder if Camren had sent them away.

When Espen's hand settled on Jacob's shoulder, Jacob thought she knew why no one had noticed her. "You're not going to tell me--" she began, turning to face the older Healer as the bustle of the castle swarmed around them.

"I'm not going to tell you a single thing," Espen said. "I'm only going to congratulate you for keeping a level head through all of this. Bernadette would like to see you if you have a moment."

"I just wanted to make sure they were okay," Jacob said.

Espen's eyes flashed, but only for a moment. "I believe they will be fine," she said. "Eventually, perhaps they might find their way to the Hunt's home in Faerie, and eventually, perhaps Gabriel will take them in if they wish it so. I don't think that would be a terrible idea."

Jacob didn't think that would be a terrible idea either. "Is Bernadette the Queen?"

"Bernadette and Camren are twins," Espen said. "That's rare enough for elves, and even rarer for the ruling class. Evidently, when they assumed the throne together, only a handful of their subjects thought they would succeed. So far, they've not torn the kingdom apart."

"Why would they get involved in this?" Jacob asked. "Or were they just looking for us?"

"They only needed an excuse to get involved," Espen said. "And you and Danny provided them with that excuse."

Jacob peered at the Hounds again, who were eating now, carefully, giving no one any cause to denounce them as uncivilized. But she noticed Robin shooting glances at Noah here and there, as if to help him remember how to pretend to be human again.

"I'll speak to Bernadette," she said. "But what does she want to talk to me about?" She hadn't yet asked why Sennet hadn't come to find her, and that worried her more than she cared to admit. "Arlen *is* okay, isn't he? And nothing *else* happened?"

"Amalea and Nathaniel found Arlen lying where you left him, and he, in turn, told them what he knew when he woke up," Espen said as they walked down the hall. "They took him to Sennet's house, but since Amalea knew where you and Danny had ended up, she thought it best to contact her cousins." Espen smiled. "Nathaniel did not tell Arlen he was a Hound, at first. Sennet thought it best that he not know. He was confused, poor child."

"I was confused, too," Jacob admitted. "The Darkbrook here was different enough to be confusing, and the Hounds--I can't believe the Council would do such a thing--"

Espen stopped in front of a wooden door and knocked. An elf Jacob didn't recognize opened the door, bowed, and motioned them inside.

It was the library again, but through a different door this

time. Or maybe it was a different library; Jacob didn't see the mirror they'd crossed through, or nearly as many books.

Bernadette sat at a long banquet-style table with two familiar people--Sennet and Arlen, who still looked a bit pale, but smiled when he saw Jacob.

"I'm glad you're okay," he said.

"And I'm glad they found you," Jacob said. "If they hadn't, we would still be stuck in Darkbrook without any food or water."

"I took the liberty of ordering tea and some sandwiches, since my brother is busy feeding the Hounds," Bernadette said. "I'm sure you must be hungry as well."

Jacob accepted a plate of sandwiches and a cup of tea that smelled faintly flowery and sat where Bernadette indicated. She wasn't really hungry until she bit into a sandwich and realized she hadn't eaten any lunch in her panic to find the Hounds.

"I heard you did a very good job at keeping everyone alive," Sennet said, smiling at her. "And Camren told me your portal was flawless. Your uncle will be proud."

"Uncle Lucas won't want to let me out of his sight ever again," Jacob said. "What did he say? You *did* tell him--"

"I think your uncle is beginning to realize that by being a Healer, you're going to end up in situations that aren't quite safe, or situations like this one will find you," Espen said. "Of course, we had no intention of sending you off by yourself quite yet, but Freda was desperate, and we understand that. She merely wanted to fulfill her promise to the Hounds." She glanced at Sennet. "Or redeem herself."

"What happens now?" Jacob asked. "Have you spoken to the Council yet?"

Bernadette glanced at Arlen. "There *is* no Council. Arlen has never seen them; his uncle claims to meet them in secret, and although there are rumors, they all go back to Simon Parker and no one else."

"What did the Hunt ever do to *him*?" Jacob asked, remembering the hatred in his gaze. And then she remembered what Espen had said. "What do you mean, *redeem* herself?"

"We took the liberty of searching the building for anything he might have been searching for," Bernadette said. "And we found quite a bit, other than the library, which he tried to burn."

"Quite a bit of what?" Jacob asked. "And Noah put out the fire--"

"The fire only destroyed a few shelves of books, and Noah's spell did not damage the others," Espen said. "He seems to have learned quite a bit of fine control; it will be interesting to see what he does with the rest of his life."

"But what we think Arlen's uncle was looking for actually was in the cellars, and I doubt the Hunt had much use for the cellars." She glanced up as the door opened again, and Camren ushered in the two Hounds, who were dressed in clothing obviously borrowed, but no less fine than what Camren wore himself.

They'd taken baths, too, because Robin's hair was still damp and Noah's had turned from dirty blond to almost white. Save for the color of his eyes, he could have been Josiah's twin.

"Did you know about the treasure in the cellars?" Bernadette asked as soon as they sat down.

"The treasure in the cellars?" Noah repeated, and shook his head. "I don't think I've ever *been* in the cellars--"

"I knew it was there," Robin said, and folded his arms. "Is that what he wanted? The treasure?"

"What kind of treasure?" Jacob asked.

"When Darkbrook was abandoned, they didn't actually pack; they fled. Since the Council was all dead, no one actually knew what they'd left behind. Over the years, certain stories had surfaced about a fantastical treasure inside the forest; we think that perhaps Arlen's uncle had actual proof. A journal, or papers, or something like that." Bernadette smiled. "I sent a few elves to Simon Parker's house to see what they could find. They found quite a bit."

"You can't eat treasure," Noah said softly.

"That's true," Espen said, her voice equally soft. "And you cannot bargain with it, either." She hesitated. "Healers are not infallible. We are human. And Freda had been watching the binding for *years*--since it was created."

"What kind of treasure?" Jacob asked again. "Are you saying that Freda--"

Robin dug into a pocket of his borrowed pants and pulled out something that sparkled and shone, even in the palm of his hand. It wasn't very big; just a flat sparkly stone, but it shone with a light of its own like no other stone would shine.

He set it on the table. "I thought it might be useful," he said into the silence. "It kept me warm, too."

Jacob reached out and touched the stone. It *was* warm, pulsing, almost, as if it held some sort of life of its own. "That's a dragon stone," she said, remembering now where she'd seen them before. "The dragons use them for light."

"It's also a special kind of diamond," Bernadette said. "And there are *hundreds* of them in Darkbrook's cellars."

"I didn't count," Robin said. "There was gold, too, in boxes."

"We found that as well," Bernadette said. "Although the question of who *hired* Simon Parker to eliminate the Hunt was a more difficult--"

"I thought there might be stores of food," Robin admitted. "We didn't have much use for sparkly stones or gold."

Neither Hound seemed to hear what Espen and Bernadette weren't quite saying out loud, but Jacob was beginning to have an idea. "Freda and Arlen's uncle were working together?"

Noah reached out to touch the stone, and then with a glance at Robin, he lifted it and turned it this way and that, the sparkles reflecting across his face. "When Arlen's uncle appeared, he shot Freda first," he said. "And he said something about--"

"'How dare you betray me'?" Robin said. "I thought he was talking to Arlen, at first, but that didn't make sense. For all he knew, Arlen wasn't with us by choice."

"I'm sorry," Espen said to the Hounds. "We believe she hired him with promises of the treasure if he killed your Master. I don't believe he was supposed to kill you all."

Jacob remembered what Sennet had said, back when they were at the mall. "Healers aren't perfect."

Sennet smiled sadly. "Unfortunately so."

"But we think she intended to do the right thing, in the end," Espen said. "She had every intention of sending you to safety. That doesn't condone her actions, but--"

"It helps," Noah said quietly. "Thank you for telling us."

"The Council must have made some sort of bargain with the dragons to get that many stones," Bernadette said to change the subject. "Perhaps they thought it would be easier to light the halls with these instead of magic. Or perhaps they intended to use them somewhere else. Either way, they've been stored in the cellars for over a hundred years, and regardless of what anyone promised Arlen's uncle, the treasure is still intact."

"Who owns it now?" Arlen asked.

"Well, that's a good question," Bernadette said, and smiled again. "There is no Council, the Hunt is gone--"

"By right of conquest, the treasure belongs to you," Espen said, staring directly at the Hounds. "No one else has a legitimate claim."

Noah stared at her, and then at the stone in his hand. "No."

"Not by right of conquest," Robin said.

"We have no use for treasure," Noah said, carefully placing the stone back onto the table, where it sparkled and glittered and shone.

They owned nothing, these Hounds, not even the clothes they wore. And yet even though they owned nothing, *had* nothing, they wanted nothing to do with Darkbrook's treasure. Jacob wondered if she'd feel the same way if she were in their place.

"The treasure cannot stay in Darkbrook's cellars," Bernadette said. "Eventually, word would get out, and--"

"The treasure was intended for Darkbrook," Noah said. "Why can't it be used for Darkbrook now?"

Robin nodded. "Your Veil passes through the binding; how difficult would it be for you to take control of the entire forest? You could open Darkbrook as the Council first intended, and--"

"And use the treasure to run it properly," Noah said, fairly bouncing with excitement.

Jacob risked a glance at Espen, who was smiling, and at Camren, who was positively grinning. Arlen smiled; Sennet nodded; only Bernadette seemed shocked.

"It is a *lot* of treasure, and you are due some compensation for your losses," she finally said. "Surely--"

"Do we *need* money where we're going?" Robin asked.

"Well, some," Jacob said. "You'll have to buy more clothes, and food to eat." Although she wasn't sure about the food; she doubted the Wild Hunt ever went grocery shopping, and there was plenty of game in the forest.

"So maybe we could take just some of the treasure and leave the rest to Darkbrook," Noah suggested.

"I think that would be--fine," Bernadette said. "Espen, *can* we reopen Darkbrook?"

"I think Darkbrook would be best served in your capable hands," Espen said. "The binding is gone; the forest is open for the first time in over a hundred years. And it is yours for the taking. I doubt anyone will challenge your rule."

"We'll have to figure out a way to expand the Veil to the edge of the forest," Camren said, staring at the glowing diamond in the middle of the table. "And--"

"Why don't you go talk to your friends," Bernadette suggested. "Get them started on this before the rest of Simon's hunters decide to look for him and find the binding gone."

Camren nodded, already distracted. "I will do that." He snagged a sandwich from the plate, nodded to everyone, and hurried out the door.

Only a moment after that, Danny arrived, looking a bit breathless. "They told me you were here--"

"You're not interrupting," Espen said. "Part of this concerns you as well. Sit down."

Danny sat beside Jacob and smiled at her. She smiled back, glad to see him happy now that he'd found his family.

"Would you like a cup of tea?" Bernadette asked and lifted the teapot.

"Thank you," Danny said, and accepted a cup.

Bernadette refilled everyone else's cup as well, leaving Jacob to wonder just how much a teapot like that could hold.

"Now. My brother will keep himself busy with the Veil and Darkbrook, and I also have some things to take care of--and it's getting late. I would be honored if you would spend the night here--again--and we can talk more in the morning."

"Sennet and I have lodging to arrange for you both as well, and news to report," Espen said. "My tasks might take more than a day, but I will return as quickly as I can."

"There's more than one library," Bernadette said, "and you all are welcome to their contents."

"Are you going to leave with your family?" Jacob asked

Danny, who hesitated before shaking his head.

"No, they went back home," he said. "They'll be back--some of them--tomorrow afternoon. They have some things to take care of as well, and it wasn't anything I could help with." He glanced at Jacob, and then at the Hounds. "And anyway, I meant what I said. I didn't want to leave you hanging."

"Arlen, it's up to you. Do you want to stay here or come back with me?" Sennet asked. "I'll be back when Espen returns; a day at most."

"You are welcome to stay," Bernadette said when he didn't answer.

"I'll stay," he finally said.

With that, Espen and Sennet took their leave, and Sennet gave Jacob an encouraging smile as she passed. Jacob smiled back, pleased that everything had gone so well, but also a bit apprehensive nonetheless. For the Hounds, the future was a wide open book with a million pages. For Danny, reunion with his family. For her--

"There is one last thing," Sennet said on her way out the door.

"What's that?" Bernadette asked.

"We also have to decide what to do about Freda's house," Espen said. "Traditionally, it would go to the Healer in charge of this--"

Jacob stared at her. "What? Not me!" But still--an actual Healer's house? Like Sennet's? And Espen's? Ophelia would be beside herself with joy.

"But since Jacob is still in school and not quite a full member of the Healer's network yet, we've decided to--"

"As you said, traditionally it would go to the Healer in charge of this," Danny said, daring to interrupt. "And I think that Jacob deserves--"

"Wait, wait, wait," Sennet said, laughing. "You needn't jump to her defense. Jacob is almost fifteen years old. I received my house and status in the Healer network when I was seventeen, and I *was* the youngest."

"We've decided to let Jacob decide," Espen finished before anyone else could interrupt. "It's a big responsibility, having your own house. And since it is a *Healer's* house, it's an even *bigger* responsibility."

Jacob stared at both Healers. "Would...would I have to stay here?"

Sennet shook her head. "Healers houses are a bit like portals in their own right," she said. "They tend to exist in a few places at once. You wouldn't have to stay here. In fact, Minerva's apprentice is looking for an assignment, and this might be perfect for her. But you could visit if you want to--"

"And if Danny's family decides to stay here instead of petition to move back to *our* world, he could visit whenever he wished," Espen said. "And so could you."

Danny let out a breath. "That's good to know," he said, and Jacob wondered if that was part of the stuff he had mentioned that he couldn't help his family with. "They like it here."

"Were you thinking about staying?" Bernadette asked.

"Well--" Danny glanced at Jacob, then looked away. "I would miss the friends I've made, and I would miss Jacob. And I didn't know what to do. But if I can visit whenever I want, my mother would be very happy."

As far as Jacob knew, he was still living in Mr. Moore's spare bedroom, and both Mr. Moore and Danny seemed happy with the situation there. Now that he'd found his family, she thought that perhaps he would settle in a bit more and not be so much of a stranger.

"I'd miss you, too," she said. "And I'm sure Josiah would as well."

"Of course you don't have to decide now," Espen said. "Get some rest. We'll take you to see the house when we get back."

Outside the library door, the bustle of the castle seemed to have lessened a bit; only one elf had passed since Espen had opened the door. The halls seemed quieter, too, as if the castle itself was settling down to sleep.

Noah yawned and tried to hide it with one hand.

"You're tired," Bernadette said. "Why don't you all go to

sleep? Arlen, I'll show you to your room. Danny, are you staying the night?"

"Yes, but I'm not picky," Danny said. "I can sleep anywhere."

Bernadette laughed. "We'll find you a bed."

Both Sennet and Espen were gone now, with a final smile to Jacob, who felt a bit numb with all of the surprises. But she didn't say a word when Noah and Robin stood and Robin drained the rest of his tea, or when Bernadette delivered Arlen into the care of a waiting elf.

"The room I've been sleeping in is right next to Noah and Robin's room," Jacob said.

"And there's an empty room right next to theirs," Bernadette suggested. "I had it aired out a bit earlier, just in case we would need it. Danny, you can sleep there. Arlen's in the room across the hall. I'm sure by now you know the way."

She saw them off and they walked together down the hall, silent until they reached their respective rooms and both Hounds vanished inside.

"Are you sure you wouldn't rather stay?" Jacob asked. "I can still come visit, and you don't have to--"

She was about to say 'come back just because of me', but Danny--after glancing both ways down the hallway to make sure they were truly alone--shook his head and smiled.

"I wanted to make sure my family was okay," he said. "And

happy. They've made a life here, and my mother doesn't really want to leave. Neither do my sisters or brothers. But if I can visit--that will be best, I think."

He didn't seem at all sad about only visiting.

"Well, don't be such a stranger, then," Jacob said. "I hardly saw you for *weeks* after everything was sorted out before. I thought maybe--" *Maybe you didn't want to be reminded about what happened,* she thought, but didn't finish the sentence out loud.

Danny shrugged. "I didn't think I'd be allowed to see you again," he said. "I thought--that I'd be punished, or banned from polite company, or--that your uncle would--"

"I can't see Uncle Lucas ordering me not to be your friend," Jacob said. "Just as I can't see Gabriel ordering Josiah never to speak to you again." She grinned at the expression on his face. "And anyway, if Uncle Lucas told me that, I don't have Josiah's problem if I decided to disobey."

"Oh," Danny said. "I see." He smiled, then, and that made her remember the first time she had met him, when she'd thought he was only a wolf and had tried to cast a ward against being eaten. "Well. Goodnight, Jacob."

"Goodnight, Danny."

And then, before she could turn away, he leaned down and kissed her--on the *cheek*--just a peck, but still, a kiss. And before she could say one word, he vanished into his room and left her standing in the hallway with what was probably a sappy smile on her face even though no one could see it.

She *almost* left it at that, then, and could have very easily gone to bed and fallen asleep. And probably dreamed of Danny. But she thought she knew what he would be thinking right now, so she knocked on his door instead.

It took him a long time to answer her knock, even though he'd *just* shut the door behind him. And when he appeared in the doorway, he didn't look happy to see her at all.

"Danny, I--"

And then a shape loomed up behind him, and Arlen's uncle grinned over his shoulder.

"Did you know that the elves have weapons made of silver?" he asked. "And that if you don't fetch the Hounds right away, little girl, I'll murder your sweetheart? Don't think I didn't see. And if you even *try* to sound the alarm--"

Jacob took a step back. "How did you--"

"Escape?" Arlen's uncle laughed softly. "The elves aren't used to holding human wizards. Now. Bring the Hounds."

Jacob heard a door open, somewhere nearby. It was a faint enough sound for it to be the Hounds' door, and she could only hope that they had heard Arlen's uncle's voice and realized what had happened.

"Are you sure that's a good idea?" she asked. "If you have four of us as hostages, that's two *more* people you have to keep track of. If you only have two hostages--"

"Who said anything about hostages?" Arlen's uncle asked. "I intend to kill the Hounds, child. *You* will create a portal for me to escape this place, and your friend here will come with me to ensure my freedom."

Danny held himself very stiffly as Arlen's uncle pulled him back into the room. He glanced to the right, then the left, as if asking if there were elves in the hallway, and Jacob started to shake her head.

"Don't waste time, child," Arlen's uncle snapped. "Fetch the Hounds." He closed the door, leaving Jacob alone in the hallway.

Numbly, Jacob walked the short way to the Hounds' room. She knocked on the door, then opened it when they didn't answer.

Their room was empty. She felt that first, and also, the faintest hint of magic on the edge of her senses. With a heavy heart, she walked back to Danny's room and knocked on the door again.

What could she *do?*

Arlen's uncle opened the door and pulled her inside. "Where are the Hounds?"

She didn't see Danny at first, which made her panic even more, but then she saw him lying on the bed, bound with silver wire. His eyes were closed, but they opened at her approach.

"They were gone," Jacob said. "You can go look for

yourself if you don't believe me. Their room is empty."

Arlen's uncle cursed, and for a moment, Jacob thought he would take her up on the offer and actually leave them alone to check. But then he turned on her, a dagger in his hand, and Danny tried to lift himself off the bed.

"Don't you *dare--*"

"Your portal, please," Arlen's uncle growled. "I don't have *time* to play around with you. I'll kill them later."

Jacob glanced at Danny, then turned to obey. "Where do you want to go?"

"To Darkbrook's cellars, where the treasure is hidden," Arlen's uncle ordered.

"I've never *been* to Darkbrook's cellars," Jacob said. "I've only been--"

"Then to the library, damn you!" Arlen's uncle pressed the blade of the dagger against Danny's throat. "Don't force me to kill him!"

Hardly daring to turn her back on them, Jacob placed both hands on the door and whispered the spell for the portal. She couldn't think of anywhere else to anchor it *other* than Darkbrook, and then she realized, almost as an afterthought, that she had felt that faint aftertaste of magic before, when Noah had formed the portal to the elves' library and saved their lives.

Had the *Hounds* decided they could help best if they went

to Darkbrook, too? Had they heard Arlen's uncle's plan? She could only hope and pray that if they had not, they would raise the alarm and help wouldn't be slow to arrive.

When she opened the door to Darkbrook's library, it seemed no different than before. Darker, perhaps, and colder, with the stench of smoke and ashes in the air.

Arlen's uncle pulled Danny up and pushed him forward, into Jacob. She stumbled into the library and turned to catch Danny when he fell against her.

"Were they really gone?" he asked, his voice hot against her ear.

"Yes," Jacob murmured. "They may be *here*."

Arlen's uncle pulled them apart, and pushed Danny over against the wall. He pulled a spool of silver wire from his pocket and advanced; Danny tried to squirm out of the way, but the wire already around his arms and legs prevented him from moving very far.

"Leave him alone!" Jacob begged. "Haven't you done enough?"

"Silver won't kill werewolves unless it breaks the skin," Arlen's uncle said. "They're kin to vampires in that respect. If he's careful, he'll live to see the dawn. If he's not--" He looped one end of the wire around Danny's neck and fastened it to the window crank, then gave the crank a couple of hard twists.

Danny didn't quite scream, but he whimpered, and Jacob

saw his hands clench into fists.

So she did the only thing she could think of; she ran past Arlen's uncle before he could stop her, and knelt at Danny's side. She bent down, touched his face and cast a ward to protect his skin against the silver.

"Stay safe," she whispered as Arlen's uncle pulled her away.

"Jacob!" Danny didn't dare move.

"To the cellars," Arlen's uncle ordered, and pushed Jacob out the door.

There were defensive spells, of course, that she could try, but there was also Danny to consider, and the Hounds, who were hopefully plotting something and not hidden back at the elves' castle.

With the dagger at her back--for, Arlen's uncle said, even though she was human and a Healer, what could stop him from murdering her as well?--Jacob followed his lead all the way down to the cellars, down too many steps to count and around twists and turns that were not at her Darkbrook.

What would she give to see Ash appear right now, or Emma? Or a small brown bat, rushing to her rescue?

Instead, up ahead, she saw a Hound, almost glowing in the dim light of the spell Arlen's uncle had cast.

One Hound.

Arlen's uncle stopped and grabbed her arm before she could run away. "Where is the other one?" he called, his voice harsh. "If you attempt to kill me, I'll kill your friend here, like I killed the werewolf upstairs."

"He's not dead." The voice didn't belong to either Robin or Noah; in fact, Jacob thought it was Gabriel, at first. But what would the Master of the Wild Hunt be doing *here?*

At the end of the hallway, another Hound appeared, and then another. And another. All glowing, all waiting for something Jacob couldn't see.

"There are only two of you left," Arlen's uncle said, but he sounded a bit uncertain. His hand tightened on Jacob's arm. "There are only two of you left!"

A taller figure appeared amidst the Hounds--a hawk-faced man who didn't resemble Gabriel at all, but who was, obviously, the Master of this Hunt.

"Yes," he said. "Our plan worked quite perfectly. All *I* wanted was for the binding to be destroyed; it is gone now, and we are free."

There were more Hounds now, behind their Master, appearing out of the darkness like ghosts.

And then--a growl, behind them. Arlen's uncle spun around, forgetting for a moment to keep his eye on the Master of the Hunt and his Hounds.

And there was a Hound behind them, too, a single Hound who had somehow slipped behind them, or who had been waiting in the darkness all along.

"But I...I killed you all," Arlen's uncle stammered. "I...I *killed* you!"

"Illusions are funny things," the Master of the Hunt said softly. "They tend to trick even the smartest hunters. How else were we to destroy the binding? How else could my Hunt be free?"

"But once they find out--once they realize what has happened--they'll try to bind you again," Arlen's uncle whispered. "I could...I could help you--"

The Master of the Hunt laughed. It was not a nice laugh. And Arlen's uncle started to back away, forgetting--for a moment--about the Hound behind them.

Was this the *truth?* Jacob stared at the Hounds, who flickered in the spell-light, and at their Master, who seemed solid and real. Had Noah and Robin *lied* all along?

She tried to glance back at the Hound behind them, and saw a grey wolf slip through a doorway not ten feet behind the Hound. *Danny!* And since someone had freed him--and it had to be either Noah or Robin--then was all of this an illusion as the Master of the Hunt had already said?

"You, help *us?*" The Master of the Hunt shook his head. "I don't think so. Instead, what will happen is the elves will return here, bent on finding your hostages, and you will be dead." He smiled. "And we will be gone."

The Hounds had advanced; Jacob didn't see them move,

but in one moment they were too close for comfort, growling now, softly, their teeth bared. They moved together; not quite as one, but in sync as if they'd rehearsed.

"You don't want me dead," Arlen's uncle protested. "All I came for is the treasure. If you give it to me, I won't tell anyone about this. I swear--"

"No." The Master of the Hunt seemed bored now, as if negotiating was far beneath his notice. "No. You will die. *Now.*"

The Hound behind them and the ones in front leaped, as one. Arlen's uncle pushed Jacob away from him, towards the snarling Hounds, and as she landed on the floor and curled up into a tiny ball, she *felt them jump over her,* one's foot pushed her head down; one sniffed her derisively before it vanished into the fray.

Arlen's uncle shrieked. He cast a spell; the Master of the Hunt deflected it with ease and the Hounds did not seem to notice any magic at all. He swept the dagger into an arc, catching one Hound and another with the blade, and they fell, as if they were real, but there were far too many Hounds for him to kill them all with only one dagger and nothing more.

The gray wolf slipped out of the room and hugged the edges of the hallway to get to where Jacob lay; Danny shifted shape and knelt beside her as Jacob watched Arlen's uncle try to fight the mass of Hounds.

"Are you okay?" he asked, and helped her up.

Jacob started to nod, then realized that the Master of the Hunt stood right behind them, watching as Arlen's uncle fell.

And then, the Master of the Hunt was Noah, shorter and smaller and quite a bit younger, and although a hint of his Master still shone from his gaze, he smiled at Jacob as Arlen's uncle screamed.

"Perhaps it would be best if you don't look," he said, and quite suddenly, the fury of the Hounds was gone.

Jacob didn't mean to look, but when she did, she saw Robin standing over Simon Parker's body, the dagger in his hand and blood on his lips. He spat, shuddered, and nodded to them before vanishing down the hall as a Hound, the dagger falling from his hand as he shifted shape.

"I hope they really didn't poison the creek," Danny said, and Noah's eyes widened.

But Robin reappeared only a few seconds later with a mug of water in his hand and the jug in his other hand, puzzled at their alarm. "There was water left," he said, and drank away the taste of Simon Parker's death.

"Are you okay?" Jacob asked Danny, who still held himself stiffly, as if walking hurt. There were welts crisscrossing his arms where she could see his skin, but none of them seemed life-threatening, and a thin red line where the wire Arlen's uncle had twisted around his neck had burned before her wards had protected him.

"I'll be fine," Danny said. "It's nothing a little time won't heal."

"We heard what he said," Noah said in a rush, "back at the castle. We didn't know what else to do but get here first--"

"I thought I felt something, when he sent me to get you," Jacob said. "But I wasn't sure. I thought...I thought the Hounds were real, at first."

"I told you what they were," Noah said, almost apologizing. "But I didn't know if you understood."

"I did," Jacob said, and smiled at him. "You were perfect."

Noah shivered as he stared at Simon Parker's body. "It will take a long time for me to forget our Master."

Robin stepped up beside him. "Would you like to see what Simon Parker thought was so important?"

"The treasure?" Danny asked.

"None other," Noah said. "It's still here. Robin showed me right before you arrived."

"Won't the elves--" Jacob began, trying to imagine the chaos back at the elves' castle.

"They'll figure it out eventually," Robin said. "And it isn't as if we can't leave, now that the binding is gone."

"That would have been a good plan, if your Master had lived," Danny said, and there was *almost* a question in his tone of voice. "To pretend all the Hounds had died, and then get the

Healers to destroy the binding."

"Yes, it would have been," Noah said. "But our Master wasn't one for subterfuge. Be happy for that."

They walked down the hall together, and Danny seemed a bit surprised when Jacob took his hand. But then he smiled at her, and walked a bit less stiffly into a small, narrow room that was filled to the brim with stones that only began to glow at their approach, and boxes full of gold bars, the wood rotted, the gold glittering inside.

"Another treasure," Jacob said. "There was a treasure at *our* Darkbrook, too, but it came from the Selkies, way back when Darkbrook was first built. Someone died for that treasure, too."

"Perhaps one day you could tell us that story," Robin said.

"I'd love to," Jacob replied. "But right now, why don't we go inform the elves that all is well?"

"So," Danny asked as they stood in a row in front of the door. "Have you decided?"

"About what?" Jacob asked.

"The house, of course," Noah said, and spoke the spell to open the portal.

"How can I not?" Jacob asked. "I mean, a house of my own?" She grinned at Danny. "And anyway, Danny will want to visit his family and I certainly don't want to stop him." She squeezed Danny's hand.

Hesitantly, he put his arm around her shoulders. "Thanks. That means a lot to me."

Jacob leaned her head against Danny's side and put *her* arm around his waist. It fit there perfectly, and they were still standing like that, together, when Noah opened the door and Bernadette and Camren peered worriedly through the portal, only relaxing when they saw that everyone was still in one piece.

Only then did she wonder what Arlen would think of the Hounds now that his uncle was dead. She thought, perhaps, that he might be a bit relieved to know that he was free now, just as free as the Hounds to do whatever he wished.

Perhaps he'd enroll in Darkbrook. Jacob thought he would like it there.

The End

You can find ALL our books on our website at:

http://www.writers-exchange.com

all our fantasy novels:

http://www.writers-exchange.com/category/genres/fantasy/

About the Author

Jennifer St. Clair grew up in Southern Ohio and spent most of her childhood in the woods around her home. She wrote her first novel when she was thirteen, and hasn't stopped since. She lives with her ball python, Fester, and two cats, Ash and Rowan.

In her spare time, she crochets, makes cloth dolls, collects antiques, books, and vintage clothing, and takes digital photographs with varying degrees of success.

Her *Beth-Hill series* is set in the area in America that contains many supernatural creatures: Wild Hunt, Vampires, Dragons, Faery and more.

It is part of the Universe that her *Jacob Lane Series, Karen Montgomery Series* and vampire trilogy, *The Shadow Series* are set in.

Follow all her books on her author page:
http://www.writers-exchange.com/Jennifer-St-Clair/

***If you want to read more about other books
by this author, they are listed on the
following pages...***

A Beth-Hill Novel (Stand Alone Novels)

Are creatures of the night and all manner of extramundane beings drawn to certain locations in the natural world? In the Midwestern village of Beth-Hill located in southern Ohio, the population is made up of its fair share of common citizens...and much more than its share of supernatural residents. Take a walk on the wild side in this unusual place where imagination meets reality.

Blood of the Innocents

Ten years ago, Orien, crown prince of the Seleighe, was captured by his mortal enemies, locked in a dungeon and turned into a vampire. Six years into Orien's sentence, the Healer's brother Cullen disobeyed his mistress's orders to kill him and turned him into a vampire instead, thus sealing both their fates for all eternity.

Now both Orien and Cullen are set free. But a secret only Cullen knows lies locked inside his mind, threatening to drive him mad before he can uncover the identity of a traitor--the very elf who betrayed Orien and left them both to die in darkness.

Publisher: http://www.writers-exchange.com/Blood-of-the-Innocents/

Full Moon

Werewolves change into wolves when the moon is full. But Edward's curse only allows him to be *human* when the moon is full.

Alone and despairing, Edward hides himself away from the world. He's scraped out a meager existence for himself for almost a century in the forest he's grown to love and call home. But in the depths of a terrible winter, he stumbles across clues from the life his mother left behind in Faerie. The truth may give him the answers he needs about the source of his birthright... and the curse that holds him captive.

Publisher: http://www.writers-exchange.com/Full-Moon/

Secrets When in Shadow Lie

Twelve years ago, Ryan Grey was cursed by a witch to hide a secret. He's lived with the curse of being unable to die permanently, and, over the years he's slowly losing the memory of his past until almost nothing remains.

But now, after a chance meeting with an elf named Zipporah, he discovers the key to unlocking the secret and breaking the curse once and for all...if he can survive the breaking.

Publisher:

http://www.writers-exchange.com/Secrets-When-in-Shadow-Lie/

A Beth-Hill Novel: Jacob Lane Series

Are creatures of the night and all manner of extramundane beings drawn to certain locations in the natural world? In the Midwestern village of Beth-Hill located in southern Ohio, the population is made up of its fair share of common citizens...and much more than its share of supernatural residents.

Jacob Lane is a ten-year-old girl who's spent her life unaware of her magical heritage. After being sent to Darkbrook, a school of magic, supernatural mysteries seem to spring to life all around her and her new friends.

Book 1: The Tenth Ghost

After Jacob Lane's parents mysteriously vanish, she's sent to Darkbrook, the only school of magic in the United States. While there, she and her new friends stumble upon a series of mysterious deaths in the nine ghosts that haunt the halls of Darkbrook. These ghosts were students who died at the school over the past hundred years. Will Jacob become the tenth ghost, or can she stop a witch's reign of terror?

Publisher: http://www.writers-exchange.com/The-Tenth-Ghost/

Book 2: The Ninth Guest

When Jacob's friend Ophelia's family decides to open up their castle for guests, amateur paranormal sleuth Jacob Lane is invited to join in on the fun. "Spend the night in a vampire's castle and live to tell the tale!" is supposed to be a fundraiser to help Ophelia's family pay the bills. Heating a castle costs quite a bit, after all. But, after the truth of an old secret is uncovered, what began as an innocent business venture soon turns deadly when vampire hunters get involved.

For years, the vampire hunters have had only one goal: To destroy all vampires. With the help of a new friend, Jacob and Ophelia must work together to save the entire VonBriggle family from extinction.

Publisher: http://www.writers-exchange.com/The-Ninth-Guest/

Book 3: The Eighth Room

For two hundred years, the Selkies have kept themselves separate from those who live on land. But now the Selkies need allies or they'll be crushed by their ancient enemies, the Finfolk.

Jacob and Ophelia, students at the only school of magic in the United States, uncover a mystery that dates back to Darkbrook's beginnings. While helping clean out old storage rooms for classroom expansion, they find something that might save the Selkies from extinction. With the help of the youngest member of the Wild Hunt who are no longer so wild or terrifying, they must foil the Finfolk who desire the Selkie's destruction...or die trying.

Publisher: http://www.writers-exchange.com/The-Eighth-Room/

Book 4: The Seventh Secret

After a picture of Niklas, the dragons' liaison to the only school of magic in the United States, shows up in too many newspapers to count, Darkbrook is forced to go on the defensive. The secret of Darkbrook's existence has been discovered. But there are more than dragonhunters in the forest, and, as Jacob Lane, supernatural sleuth and student at Darkbrook, learns how to use her newly discovered talent of healing, she helps to right an old wrong and must battle a teenaged wizard intent on proving--once and for all--that magic is real.

Publisher: http://www.writers-exchange.com/The-Seventh-Secret/

Book 5: The Sixth Stone

Jacob Lane, supernatural sleuth, and Danny, her werewolf friend, stumble across an alternate world where the Wild Hunt was never bound, and Darkbrook, the school of magic they attend, was abandoned a hundred years ago.

But when the Hounds of the Hunt wish to surrender, the two students are swept up in a whirlwind of heartbreak, betrayal, and the discovery of a lost treasure.

Publisher: http://www.writers-exchange.com/The-Sixth-Stone/

A Beth-Hill Novella: Karen Montgomery Series

Are creatures of the night and all manner of extramundane beings drawn to certain locations in the natural world? In the Midwestern village of Beth-Hill located in southern Ohio, the population is made up of its fair share of common citizens...and much more than its share of supernatural residents. Take a walk on the wild side in this unusual place where imagination meets reality.

Karen Montgomery was an ordinary woman until she stumbled into the extraordinary... A bargain with elves worth its weight in gold. A plague of sinister ladybugs. Rogue vampire hunters, including one who tries to turn over a new leaf--with disastrous consequences. A ghostly huntsmen of the Wild Hunt wishing for redemption. Karen's life will never be the same again.

Book 1: Budget Cuts

Karen Montgomery is used to taking care of the unpleasant jobs no one else wants to deal with. When a shortage of funds forces her to fire fifteen employees from the library, she isn't happy, but the nasty task has to be done and she is, after all, the boss. But Karen finds finishing her task impossible when she can't seem to track down Ivy Bedinghaus, a night clerk she's never actually met. Once she finally does confront Ivy, she's thrust into a centuries-old conflict that makes her previous troubles radically pale in comparison.

Publisher: http://www.writers-exchange.com/Budget-Cuts/

Book 2: The Secret of Redemption

Karen Montgomery, librarian, finds herself embroiled in another otherworldly adventure...

A member of the Wild Hunt--ghostly myths that aren't so ghostly (or myth-like) anymore--needs help in reconciling who he once was in life and who he is now.

A little girl has gone missing. And the one most likely responsible for her disappearance is the one Karen must prove innocent.

Publisher:

http://www.writers-exchange.com/The-Secret-of-Redemption/

Book 3: Ladybug, Ladybug

An innocent attempt to rid the library of a plague of ladybugs turns sinister when a rogue vampire hunter gets the contract for pest control.

Ivy Bedinghaus, who works for Karen as a night clerk--along with all the vampires in Beth-Hill--are in danger, and their only hope for survival is with the help of Karen, a member of the Wild Hunt, and Russell Moore, a reformed vampire hunter.

Publisher: http://www.writers-exchange.com/Ladybug-Ladybug/

Book 4: Detour

One wrong turn sends Karen down a road that shouldn't exist, to the site of an old accident and an even older mystery. With reformed vampire hunter Russell Moore's help, Karen finds the key to the mystery. But Russ keeps his own secrets...some of which are deadly.

When old friends from Russ' past come to call, Karen realizes his secrets might just mean his doom. After a terrible incident three years ago, before Karen met him, Russ wants only to live the rest of his life quietly in

Beth-Hill. But his secret might not allow him the new lease on life Russ longs for.

Publisher: http://www.writers-exchange.com/Detour/

Companion Story: Russ' Story: Capture

Long before Russell Moore ever met supernatural sleuth Karen Montgomery or set foot in Beth-Hill, he was a vampire hunter, possibly the best vampire hunter of all. He brought down whole nests of vampires, caring little about the consequences of his actions. Anyone who lived with or helped the vampires became enemies to be slaughtered.

So what kind of an idiot would capture a ruthless vampire hunter without a conscience and try to reform him?

Ethan Walker was that idiot. Wanting to protect his family, Ethan set out to prove to Russ that vampires weren't all evil, soulless creatures. If Russ would allow himself to witness their lives, see their humanity, surely he and other vampire hunters like him would let them live in peace. *Surely?*

Publisher: http://www.writers-exchange.com/Capture/

A Beth-Hill Novel: The Abby Duncan Series

Are creatures of the night and all manner of extramundane beings drawn to certain locations in the natural world? In the Midwestern village of Beth-Hill located in southern Ohio, the population is made up of its fair share of common citizens...and much more than its share of supernatural residents. Take a walk on the wild side in this unusual place where imagination meets reality.

Situated in Beth-Hill, where imagination meets reality, is The Rose Emporium, owned by elderly and not-a-little-odd Rose Duncan. The large Victorian house smackdab in the middle of nowhere is a cross between a pawn shop and an antique store that caters to supernatural creatures needing to barter. Rose's twenty-something niece, Abby Duncan, discovers that the world isn't made up of just run-of-the-mill, ordinary humans but an entire spectrum of unusual beings. With her preconceptions about what's normal and what's not turned upside-down, Abby is in for a whole lot of startling truths, mysteries--about herself and the people and places around her--and danger.

Novella 1: By Any Other Name

Woodturner Abby Duncan decides to sell her spindles at a local Renaissance Festival with only some success. After all, no one really spins their own yarn anymore, do they? While there, she discovers that one of her newfound friends is not what he appears--and his secret is about to get him killed!

Publisher: http://www.writers-exchange.com/By-Any-Other-Name/

Book 2: The Uncrowned Queen

Abby Duncan's elderly Aunt Rose has always been a bit odd. And now she's off on a mysterious trip, leaving Abby behind to run the Rose Emporium, an unusual sort of antique shop. Such an extraordinary store would have been a perfect place for Seth and the others, her friends from the Renaissance Festival, to take a break from traveling between Faires. But when tragedy strikes and Abby and the others discover the true nature of the Rose Emporium, they'll have to travel into Faerie itself before their tightknit group is whole again.

Abby doesn't know much about her family history, but she's about to find out the truth...whether she likes it or not.

Publisher: http://www.writers-exchange.com/The-Uncrowned-Queen/

A Beth-Hill Novel: The Shadows Trilogy

Are creatures of the night and all manner of extramundane beings drawn to certain locations in the natural world? In the Midwestern village of Beth-Hill located in southern Ohio, the population is made up of its fair share of common citizens...and much more than its share of supernatural residents. Take a walk on the wild side in this unusual place where imagination meets reality.

A Dreamer dreams the future when the past is not yet laid to rest. Ten years ago, a plague swept across the Seven Kingdoms. Ten years ago, the Queen of Iomar's son was exiled and named the author of the magical plague. Now, in the present, Terrin works to complete his ultimate goal: Control of the Seven Kingdoms using his son's power to supplement his own. But his attempt at dominion meets resistance and the fate of the world rests in the unlikely hands of an exiled prince, a Dreamer, and a vampire...

Book 1: The Prince of Shadows

When Alban's father Terrin appeared at the castle door with a vampire in tow and apologies on his lips, Alban fell under his spell just like everyone else and welcomed him home. But Terrin didn't return to live quietly in his brother's kingdom. He had other plans and, with Alban's untrained powers at his disposal, he begins his ruthless plan to destroy the Seven Kingdoms and rule them all, beginning with his brother's death.

Terrin engineers events to cast the blame on his nephew, Teluride, intending to see the boy executed for his father's murder. But there are those who would thwart Terrin in his mad plan for power, and Alban forms an unlikely alliance with Skade, the reclusive Queen of Iomar, and Terrin's slave, a young vampire with no memory of his name or origins. Although the future looks grim, Alban and the vampire attempt to stop Terrin...and they almost succeed.

A darker history lies at the heart of Terrin's treachery, and only Skade knows the true reason why Terrin would murder his own brother and attempt to destroy both Alban and the vampire to achieve his goals. The Ghost who resides in Skade's mirror--her servant and thrall--holds one of the keys to Terrin's madness. Unfortunately, more than one person wishes for the past to remain the past and the future to hold no shadows of what might have been...

Publisher: http://www.writers-exchange.com/The-Prince-of-Shadows/

Book 2: Lost In Shadows

Events set in motion ten years ago come to a head as Skade, the reclusive Queen of Iomar, and Nicodemus, who is imprisoned by Skade, struggle to free Alban and the vampire from Terrin's grasp. Old secrets come to light when Skade's exiled son is forced to face his past--or die trying to redeem himself once and for all. Can the crimes of the past truly be forgiven? Only time will tell...and time is running out.

Publisher: http://www.writers-exchange.com/Lost-In-Shadows/

Book 3: Bound In Shadows

With his power crushed, brother to the king and father to Alban, Terrin is forced to take drastic measures to regain his sons after they are freed and harness the power they possess. But he has an ally inside the healer's house where they are recovering who works to further his plans. The Queen of Iomar, Skade's son, courts redemption to try to save his mother's life, and the vampire who no longer remembers his own name dreams a dream that might save them all...or damn them if success is thwarted.

Publisher: http://www.writers-exchange.com/Bound-In-Shadows/

The Dead Who Do Not Sleep

Will Spark only wants a good night's sleep after a night of drinking. Instead, two thugs bang on his door, demanding answers to questions he can't understand. And then they killed him...

Publisher:

http://www.writers-exchange.com/The-Dead-Who-Do-Not-Sleep/

A Beth-Hill Novel: Wild Hunt Series

Are creatures of the night and all manner of extramundane beings drawn to certain locations in the natural world? In the Midwestern village of Beth-Hill located in southern Ohio, the population is made up of its fair share of common citizens...and much more than its share of supernatural residents. Take a walk on the wild side in this unusual place where imagination meets reality.

The Wild Hunt roamed the forest outside of Beth-Hill until the Council bound them for a hundred years. Nevertheless, a century of existence has made an indelible mark not easily forgotten for these ghostly myths that are no longer so ghostly or myth-like...

Book 1: Heart's Desire

The Wild Hunt roamed the forest outside of Beth-Hill until the Council bound them for a hundred years--a lifetime for a human but only a passing thought to one such as Gabriel, Master of the Wild Hunt. As the Council's binding draws to a close, old enemies reappear to ensure that the Wild Hunt is bound once more--to a creature much worse than the Council has been.

Publisher: http://www.writers-exchange.com/Hearts-Desire/

Book 2: Fire and Water

As a young vampire, Erialas Morgan brought his mother back to life with a spell that shouldn't exist, shouldn't have worked...perhaps shouldn't have been performed at all. Desperation and love are his only excuses for doing the unthinkable.

There are others who wish to use that same spell for their own gain--and to destroy the Wild Hunt once and for all. Caught in the middle of a war between the Morgan clan of vampires and their human kin, Erialas turns to the Hunt for help. But even Gabriel, the Master of the Wild Hunt, may not be able to stop the tide of death and destruction once it turns.

Publisher: http://www.writers-exchange.com/Fire-and-Water/

Book 3: The Lost

Almost sixty years ago, Darkbrook, the only school of magic in the United States, opened its doors to students of decidedly different natures, sending out letters of invitation to the elves, the dragons, and the vampires. The three who responded to the invitation banded together despite their differences but vanished only weeks later along with an entire classroom full of students and their teacher after a field trip gone horribly wrong.

The Wild Hunt has healed and the Hounds have grown closer together, keeping Darkbrook's forest safe and secure for those who live there. Malachi, one of the eldest members of the Wild Hunt, has adapted to Josiah's spell to help him see, but when a demon boy trapped in the body of a human body for sixty years inside the school disrupts the newfound calm, the Hunt--and those they protect--are thrust into a struggle that should have ended long ago when a vampire, an elf, and a dragon vanished into the Mists.

Publisher: http://www.writers-exchange.com/The-Lost/

Book 4: A Glint of Silver

Jericho is a vampire who wants is to live away from the Richmond household of vampires led by his ruthless father Connor. When Jericho tries to escape, Connor punishes him and leaves him to die. Tristan is determined to be the one to bring Jericho back, but he can't see him suffer for wanting a normal life. As long as Connor lives, Jericho will never be safe or free. As long as Connor *lives*...

Publisher: http://www.writers-exchange.com/A-Glint-of-Silver/

Book 5: All That Glitters

As a member of the cruel Morgan Household of vampires, twelve-year-old Arthur Morgan has been abused all his life.

Maya, a water fairy, shows him just how horrible and twisted the household he's grown up is. With her help, and the unexpected help of an adult vampire, Arthur attempts to escape.

Can he become something more than what his father has decreed?

Publisher: http://www.writers-exchange.com/All-That-Glitters/

The Chelsea Chronicles

Normally a quiet, serene place, Chelsea Kingdom seems like the perfect location for a centuries' old vampire to blend in and live a normal life, even escape hunters and an angry mob. Unfortunately, his timing couldn't be worse...

Book 1: So You Want to be a Vampire

Chelsea Kingdom is usually a pretty quiet place but recent murders--committed by a vampire--upset the calm. Newcomer to town, Vlad Dhalgren wants only to blend in and live a normal life. He quickly learns that isn't possible, given that other vampires have been hiding in the shadows around the castle--in plain sight--for years.

Despite her lineage, Anna Everett, the crown princess of the Kingdom of Chelsea, isn't a wizard like her father, which means she will never be Queen. She has only one friend, Valerian Moreton--Val--who has secrets he's never shared that could get him *and* Anna killed...

Publisher:

http://www.writers-exchange.com/So-You-Want-to-be-a-Vampire/

Book 2: Transformation

As Anna, crown princess of Chelsea, adjusts to life as a vampire after recent events, Vlad plans for a future he has no real hope to seeing come to pass due to injuries sustained while attempting to save Anna's life. But, as life goes on for Anna and her friend Valerian "Val" Moreton, it changes for others--some of whom are not quite what they seem...

Publisher: http://www.writers-exchange.com/Transformation/

You can find ALL our books on our website at:

http://www.writers-exchange.com

all our fantasy novels:

http://www.writers-exchange.com/category/genres/fantasy/